LUCKY ME

by
Lisa Fiedler

Clarion Books/*New York*

Clarion Books
a Houghton Mifflin Company imprint
215 Park Avenue South, New York, NY 10003
Text copyright © 1998 by Lisa Fiedler

The text is set in 11/17-point Lucida Bright.

Printed in the USA.

Library of Congress Cataloging-in-Publication Data
Fiedler, Lisa.
    Lucky me / Lisa Fiedler.
    p.   cm.
    A sequel to: Curtis Piperfield's biggest fan.
    Summary: Continues the struggles of C.C. to be
her own independent self while also keeping up with
her friends at school and doing the things they do.
    ISBN 0-395-89131-0
    [1. Interpersonal relations—Fiction.
2. Dating (Social customs)—Fiction.
3. High schools—Fiction. 4. Schools—Fiction.]
I. Title.
PZ7.F457Lu   1998
[Fic]—dc21   98-5531
CIP
AC

BP 10 9 8 7 6 5 4 3 2 1

For Shannon.
And for Jennifer, Gina, and Thomas DeLuca, who
remind me what it's like to be young.

Chapter 1

I am having a dream: I am alone in the gymnasium of St. Bernadette's School for Girls; and it's not as if I'm just early for phys. ed. or I'm cutting through on my way to chapel—it's different. In the dream, I am completely and totally *alone.*

I see that I'm holding something, and I know right away it's a poem; so I suppose I'm looking for Sister Jude Thaddeus, my freshman English teacher. But she's not in the gym, because, as I said, I'm alone. It's weird and quiet, and there's this dream-fog effect, and I feel as if I'm looking at myself through the wrong end of binoculars.

Suddenly there's a commotion at center court, so I head toward the middle of the gym, still holding my poem. At first all I see is this peach-colored blur. Then as I get closer, the blur materializes into Kelly Sinclair, so now I'm no longer alone—although, being that it's Kelly, I wish I were. My first dream instinct is to run, but I can't get my feet to move except toward Kelly, who, by the way, is wearing the same obnoxiously perky peach dress she wore when Cluck took her to the Spring Formal. The dress is not even *wrinkled!* That is so Kelly.

I notice she is holding something out to me, and I squint, trying to see what it is. It appears to be a tumbleweed—a maroon-and-white plastic tumbleweed to be exact. I keep walking because, naturally, I'm curious, and then the noise begins. It's some kind of song or chant, and it's building in enthusiasm. There's also a lot of giggling, and that is what tips me off—the giggling. The tumbleweed, I now understand, is *not* a tumbleweed, but one of Kelly Sinclair's ever-present cheerleading pompoms.

It's at this point that the dream officially becomes my worst nightmare, because suddenly, I know precisely why I'm in St. Bernadette's gym: *I, Cecily Carruthers, am at cheerleading tryouts!*

* * *

I wonder if all poets wake up reaching for their journals. I do *not* wonder if all poets keep journals, as I believe this is a requirement if you call yourself by that title: Poet. Not that I actually call myself a poet out loud. It's something I feel and do, and I think that if you feel and do something often enough, it's no longer necessary to say much about it. At least, that's my take on poetry. Cheerleaders, I'm certain, have an entirely different outlook on what they do. But then, I'm about as different from cheerleaders as it's possible to be. They do things as a pack, in uniform, in unison. I prefer a more individual approach.

I suppose this is the reason I find the dream so objectionable. But I write it down anyway, close the journal, and slip out of bed. Summer is calling. Unfortunately, there's still half a day of school left.

* * *

Homeroom on the last day of school—need I say more? Sister Beatrice Anne is trying to shut us up, but it's a lost cause. I see five or six girls here who aren't even *in* my homeroom. At St. Bernadette's for Girls, the opportunities for anarchy are few and far between; we take what we can get.

St. Bernie's is your typical all-girls Catholic high school. By typical I mean that we wear hideous plaid skirts, and we get a good dose of religious education on top of the secular stuff like math and English. On the upside, we do get a lot of days off—Ascension Thursday, for example, and the Feast of the Immaculate Conception. The fact that we're expected to know what these holy days represent is actually a small price to pay.

I'm waiting for Grace Boccaluzzo to finish signing my yearbook. Grace is the kind of girl who likes to embellish; she could never just write, *Dear C.C., History was fun. See you over the summer, Love Grace.* Most likely, she is recording every single thing we've said, done, and thought since September. I think this is her way of proving to herself that it all actually took place.

Grace is the closest thing I have to a best friend at St. Bernadette's; my *real* best friends are Gilbert "Cluck" McNally, who goes to our brother school, St. Simon Peter's Boys' Prep, and Natalie Russell, who goes to Miltondale Junior High. Grace and I became best at-school friends near the beginning of the year. It was a right-place-at-the-right-time kind of friendship. I guess we both felt stuck here, surrounded by the Kelly-esque, and we bonded, Grace and I.

Grace has been signing my yearbook for what seems like three days now, filling the whole inside front cover. My guess is that she'll be signing the inside front covers of a lot of yearbooks today—although not necessarily by invitation. She likes the idea of being everyone's best buddy. She's not, of course. But I guess she thinks if she can make it *look* that way, people will accept it as truth. I imagine that thirty years from now, someone like Corinne Halihan (Captain, Varsity Field Hockey) is going to open her yearbook, read the inside front cover, and ask herself, "Who in the name of God is Grace Boccaluzzo?"

Grace dates my friend Cluck, one of the two most dateable boys from St. Simon Peter's. (Guess who dates the other one—Patrick O'Connell. Me.) I should mention that before Cluck started dating Grace, he was in love with me. Cluck and I have been best friends since kindergarten. The love thing was always a little tricky, but we worked around it.

I glance over at Grace, who is writing a tad insanely. I can see it now—all doodles and extra o's. *This year was sooooooo unbelievable. This summer will be sooooooo cool.* And every other word is probably Cluck—*Grace 'n Cluck. Thanks for fixing me up with Cluck. You and Patrick and Cluck and I are going to have sooooooo much fun.* I should stop her now. I already know what she's going to write; why waste the ink?

"Done yet?" I ask.

Grace shakes her head. She has terrifically long, dark hair, which wraps around her face so that she looks as if she's hiding. I, by comparison, could never hide in my hair. It's the kind of pinkish blonde people generally associate with strawberries—don't ask me why—and it only reaches the tops of my shoulders. Besides, I don't go in much for hiding.

Watching Grace as she scribbles down so much information makes me realize that ninth grade has been an experience I'll never forget. For one thing, I found out I am excellent at writing poetry. I found this out from Sister Jude, my favorite teacher. I also French kissed a boy for the first time this year—one of the defining moments of my life. I had this *crush,* and you'll have to believe me when I tell you that it was The Crush from Hell, because: A) It had been going on since I was in sixth grade, B) The boy, Curtis Piperfield, is a grade younger, and C) Curtis hardly knew I was alive.

I'm over Curtis now, but I still think he was very crush-worthy. He's extremely cute, and he used to play the electric guitar, and since he lives right across the street, he was not only geographically desirable, but highly visible as well. Anyway, St. Bernadette's Spring Formal was coming up and I wanted to ask Curtis (even though I knew he liked a girl named Bridget Glenn). I went to his house, and it was the weirdest thing. Some strange force just took me over, and the next thing I knew it was me up against Curtis—my lips, his tongue—and everything was one big French blur!

That kiss made me sort of famous (not exactly a good thing, believe me) since I was the very first in my group of friends to French kiss a boy. The surprising thing was, it didn't make me feel any closer to Curtis. In fact, it pretty much brought the crush to a screeching halt. Not a problem. The very next day, I found myself falling for Patrick. Patrick had already fallen for me. We wound up going to the formal together, and soon after we became—and to this day officially remain—an item.

The P.A. comes on, with an ear-rupturing sound.

HI, EVERYBODY! a voice bubbles through the static. THIS IS KELLY SINCLAIR. HERE'S A REMINDER FOR ANYONE INTERESTED IN TRYING OUT FOR THE ST. SIMON PETER'S CHEERLEADING SQUAD.

Grace looks at me. I look at Grace.

Kelly giggles into the mike, and we hear the sound echoing in the hallway. THE FIRST PRACTICE WILL

TAKE PLACE TODAY AFTER SCHOOL. TRYOUTS WILL BE HELD NEXT FRIDAY. IF YOU HAVE ANY QUESTIONS, SEE ME OR LISA BRUNO OR SISTER JUDE.

I feel my stomach tighten. What's Sister Jude got to do with cheerleading? Nothing, I hope.

"I thought Sister Maureen was the cheerleading advisor," Grace whispers.

So did I. I will have to look into this. If Sister Jude has sold out to the pep squad, I swear I will never show her another poem as long as I live.

Then the bell rings and we're off to chapel for convocation. Grace and I nearly crash into Kelly, who is just coming out of the main office with her pompoms. She gives us this big, cheerleadery smile.

The size of her smile is directly proportionate to the amount of hatred Kelly has been harboring for Grace since the formal, which was when Grace—to everyone's surprise, especially her own—stole Cluck from Kelly. I'm not sure if Grace has caught on yet that Kelly hates her. I, on the other hand, am well aware of how much Kelly despises me (partly because Cluck loved *me* first, but mostly because I don't genuflect to cheerleaders). The difference is that *I* couldn't care less.

Then Sister Jude appears behind Kelly, coming out of the office with a stack of catalogues. From where I'm standing, they look very much like the sort of catalogues from which an advisor might order new cheerleading sweaters.

"Hello, C.C."

"Hi."

She doesn't even attempt to hide the catalogues, and this bothers me a lot. She, of all people, should know that ordinary mortals can turn into pillars of salt just by looking at cheerleading catalogues. At the very least, we can get nauseated by them—which, at the very least, I suddenly am.

"I hope you'll be writing over the summer," she says.

I nod.

"Stop by anytime. I'd love to see whatever you're working on."

"Sure."

Then she gives me a smile. "I don't suppose I'll be seeing you at cheerleading tryouts?"

I shake my head. (Was there ever any doubt?)

"Have a wonderful vacation, C.C."

"Thank you, Sister." My voice is chilly. *Traitor.*

She shifts the catalogues to her other arm and walks off. It takes me a minute to get my feet going. I am trying to imagine what sin Sister Jude is trying to atone for. What other reason could she possibly have for taking up with cheerleaders?

Grace is laughing.

I say, "What?"

"Nothing."

"You're laughing. What's funny?"

Grace shrugs. "You. A cheerleader."

I laugh now, but it sounds strangled. "As if . . ."

"Kelly, yes. Natalie, maybe. Even me . . ."

"You?"

Another shrug. "But you . . ." She's really cracking up now.

"Don't hurt yourself, Grace."

I will fully admit to hating cheerleading and all that it implies. But Grace finding it so hilarious, not to mention unbelievable, that Sister Jude would consider me a potential cheerleader, is a little offensive.

"Cluck says all girls want to be cheerleaders, deep down."

"Cluck's a regular psychoanalyst," I tell her. "Deep down."

"In all the old movies, the cheerleader always gets the guy."

"There's a word for that: *Cliché.*" Actually, there are two words for that. The other one is *stupid.* "Besides, life is not an old movie." We walk a few steps in silence. There's a question I have to ask, though I'm not sure I want to hear the answer. "Do you want to be a cheerleader?"

"I don't not want to," she says.

I loathe double negatives almost as much as cheerleaders. Suddenly I'm in a hurry to get to chapel. In chapel, Grace won't be able to tell me she won't not go to tryouts, or that she doesn't not think Cluck wouldn't not love it.

"The uniform . . ." she tells me in a conspiratorial tone. "I think I wouldn't mind wearing the uniform."

I give Grace a long, purposeful, up-and-down look to remind her that she, like the other seven hundred and thirteen girls in the building, is at this very moment wearing a uniform. But maybe for her it's not the idea of wearing *a* uniform so much as wearing *another* uniform . . . *that* uniform. This strikes a chord of sympathy in me, but I'm not sure why.

We take our seats in the very last row, and I spot Kelly, who, naturally, is seated in the first row. There's this shaft of sunlight streaming through one of the stained-glass windows. The sunbeam falls on Kelly—just Kelly—and lights up her whole face.

And don't not think I didn't not see the symbolism in that.

School is over at 12:45 today. Patrick is waiting for me outside, in front of the statue of St. Bernadette. Girls stop in their tracks to look at him (which I like); Lisa Bruno actually goes over to talk to him. She looks a little embarrassed when I join them. Good.

Pat says, "Hi, C.C." He is utterly picturesque, with his peridot-green eyes and glistening, wheat-colored hair. And don't even get me started on his muscles. I'd like to jump him on the spot. So would Lisa, I can tell.

"I'm having a party next Friday night," says Lisa. "I was just telling Pat that you two are invited."

Lisa passed me in the hall two or three hundred times today; she couldn't have mentioned this to *me?*

"And invite Natalie," she says, "in case Frankie forgets."

Natalie has very successfully crossed the treacherous border between public and parochial school popularity, and I'm proud of her for it. She gets invited to a lot of parties this way. I should also mention that Lisa knows as well as I do that her brother Frankie would never forget to invite Natalie—not in a million years.

12

"I'll tell her," I assure Lisa.

She says good-bye to Pat, and takes off to join Kelly on the side lawn, where cheerleading sign-ups have begun. They are giggling already.

Pat leans over and kisses me on the cheek, then takes my backpack. The action is vintage Pat—old-fashioned, knightly. I can carry the backpack myself, of course, but Pat's way of thinking is that this is Boyfriend Territory, so I don't object.

"What do you think about cheerleaders?" I ask him.

He looks at me a moment. I suppose he thinks it's a trick question. "I don't think about cheerleaders," he tells me. "I think about you."

This is a good answer, but for some reason, it doesn't thrill me as much as you might expect.

"Well . . . what about *before* you started thinking about me?"

"C.C., I've been thinking about you for a long time." He gives me a smile he saves for moments like this—a sexy, distracting smile. It almost works, but I've got to know.

"What do you think about cheerleaders?" I ask again.

"I guess it depends on which particular cheerleader you want me to think about."

(Did I say I wanted him to think about a particular cheerleader? No.)

"I'm asking your opinion of cheerleaders in general, of the whole cheerleader concept."

Pat shrugs. "In general, I guess I'd have to say cheerleaders are okay. Can we go now?"

"Yes."

We begin walking. He takes my hand. "Wanna go for sodas?"

I don't, actually. I'd rather go to my house so we can kiss for a while before my mom comes home. She's a kindergarten teacher at Central Catholic Grammar School, and she gets home an hour later than I do, even on half days. The rules in my house about having a boy over when I'm alone have loosened up considerably since the formal. This has everything to do with the fact that Patrick is a gentleman.

Kissing Patrick will get my mind off cheerleaders, I can promise you that. I am about to tell him this when I notice something that stops me dead. On the side lawn, Lisa Bruno and Kelly Sinclair are lining up this year's harvest of cheerleading hopefuls. One of them is Grace Boccaluzzo.

And she is giggling.

Chapter 2

I am three steps ahead of Patrick the entire walk home. I tend to rush when I'm angry.

"Wait up," he calls. But I keep walking. Fast.

When we get to my house I am already warm and out of breath, and we haven't even started kissing yet. I open the front door and say, "Grace. A cheerleader."

"Grace is a cheerleader?" Pat dumps my backpack.

"Not yet," I mutter. Actually, *mutter* is inaccurate; *snarl* is more like it. "Not yet," I snarl.

"Is that why you're upset?"

I don't answer. We go to the family room, which is where our best kissing usually takes place, but I don't think Pat realizes that any and all making-out activities are on the verge of being canceled for today. He sits on the couch and waits for me to join him. I don't.

He looks at me. I look at him. *Now* he realizes, and I'm sure he is thinking: Prime kissing opportunity—wasted. I'm thinking: Grace. A cheerleader. And Pat knows it. He grins.

"Were you frightened by a cheerleader as a child?"

"Funny."

"It's nothing personal, you know."

"Grace going out for cheerleading is nothing personal?" I put my hands on my hips. "She's supposed to be my best friend."

"Cluck's supposed to be your best friend," he corrects me. "Then Natalie."

"At school," I tell him. "Grace is my best at-school friend. Cheerleaders give me a headache. I'd assumed they bugged her, too. She mentioned something this morning, but I never thought . . ."

"We could be kissing," Pat reminds me.

But I don't feel like kissing. This is very strange because, in case you hadn't guessed, I happen to enjoy kissing Patrick a lot. Who wouldn't? But betrayal and confusion don't exactly get my kissing juices going. Suddenly, there is nothing I want more on this earth than to have Patrick understand what I'm feeling. Ideally, I'd like him to understand it without me explaining it to him, and I tell myself he probably would, except that presently his mind is clouded over by the fact that he's not being kissed.

I will myself to be patient. "Did you ever wonder what it's like to be a cheerleader?"

"Never."

"They go to practice together. They go to games together. They have car washes in the parking lot . . . together."

"What's your point?"

I frown, because I already made it. "Together," I say, a bit sharply. "They do everything in sync. Sync is their life."

"Sink?"

"*Sync.* Short for synchronized. It means doing stuff together."

"I'd like to get in sync right now," he teases, "with you."

Irresistible. I sit down beside him, and we get down to kissing. After a minute or so, I forget about Grace and cheerleading altogether. Patrick O'Connell, I should mention, is the most fantastic kisser in the world. Since the Spring Formal, Pat and I have gotten very, very good at kissing each other, which may not sound like a problem, but for two kids who happen to be Catholic, it can get a little complicated.

We kiss for quite a while. Then Pat touches a button on my shirt. "What about today, C.C.?" he whispers.

I say, "I don't think so."

Pat lets out a long rush of breath, which says a lot. I feel bad, so to compensate, I give him an extremely sexy, sophisticated kiss. As it turns out, this only makes things worse.

"Are you sure?" Pat whispers.

The scary thing is, I'm not. So I change the subject. "I think Cluck put her up to it."

"What?"

"I think Cluck wants Grace to be a cheerleader."

"That's their business," says Pat, kissing me again. "Anyway, it's time."

I don't get it. "It's *time?*"

"We've been together almost three months," he tells me. "Come on, C.C. Aren't you even curious?"

"About Cluck and Grace?" I'm playing dumb, of course. (I told you it was complicated.)

Pat touches my shirt button again. "About me and you."

"Oh. That."

Curious doesn't begin to describe what I'm feeling. If you must know, I'm *desperately* curious, *scandalously* curious—even more curious than I was about kissing—and if you don't think that's frightening, then you aren't Catholic.

"Next time," I promise.

So Pat goes back to kissing. He is, as ever, a gentleman, which makes it even harder to say next time. Talk about irony.

Now *he* gives *me* an extremely sexy and sophisticated kiss.

I hear myself say, "All right."

"Are you sure?"

Again, not sure at all. But I nod and Pat's hand goes back to the button. Right now, I could care less if Grace Boccaluzzo became the Lord High Exalted Cheerleader of All Cheerleaders in the Universe.

The button is undone. I'm shaking. So is Pat.

"Okay?"

"Okay."

He moves to the next one, adding a whole new dimension to the already fabulous experience of kissing.

"Okay?"

"Okay."

Not okay. My mother is coming through the front door!

I freeze. Pat freezes. Then we thaw and shoot to opposite ends of the sofa. I finish buttoning my shirt just as Mom pokes her head into the family room. She smiles.

"Hi, kids."

"Nice to see you, Mrs. Carruthers," says Pat. He has those prep school manners my mom finds delightful. Usually, he stands up when she enters the room, but—well, you figure it out.

"Nice to see you, too," Mom says. "Hey, have you kids gotten to second? . . ."

I almost choke. *"What?"*

"I said, have you kids got a second? I have groceries in the car, and I could use a hand."

"Oh," I say, regaining composure. "Sure."

I follow Mom, and Pat follows me. She hands us each two plastic sacks of groceries, then goes around to the other side of the car for her book bag and all her teacher stuff. Construction paper goes in and out of our house like oxygen.

We go to the kitchen to drop the groceries.

Pat sighs. "That was close."

I'm not clear on his reference—close, we almost got caught, or close, we almost got to second base.

Maybe it's a double entendre. (I am a poet; double entendres intrigue me, even on the last day of school.)

I manage a smile. "Sorry."

"Me, too."

"Burger place?"

"Sure."

I tell my mother we're leaving, and we do, but not before she invites Pat for dinner. It's a vague invitation: Come for Dinner One Night. She's been doing this since Pat and I started going out, and One Night has yet to arrive. This is my doing. I'm not ready to have dinner with Pat and my parents. Don't get me wrong—I'm crazy about Patrick O'Connell. But to me, the dinner thing carries with it a genuine responsibility and a certain finality. There's this whole Now What? element, if you know what I mean. I believe that a boy having dinner at your house with your parents can change your relationship forever.

Halfway to the burger place, Pat asks me an interesting question: "What changed your mind?"

The most logical and honest answer is probably hormones. But I don't say that. "It seemed right," I tell him. "Didn't it seem right to you?" Stupid question.

"Lisa and Frankie Bruno's parents are going away," Pat informs me.

I'm a little surprised by this change of subject. "That's nice," I say. Then it hits me. "Oh. Away." Mr. and Mrs. Bruno are going away, and this, of course, explains Lisa's party. No parental supervision. Alcohol on the premises. It's the stuff police reports are made of.

"So maybe Friday," says Pat.

"Maybe."

We reach the burger place, which is packed. I look around and discover that the cheerleaders and would-be cheerleaders aren't there yet, but Cluck is. I give him a smile and he says, "Yow, C.C. Yow, Pat."

The sound of his voice, which is this soft, sexy rasp, makes four girls turn their heads. There is an energy force that Cluck just sort of radiates. I'm not kidding.

Frankie Bruno is there, too, and he waves us over. He tells me he called Natalie, who said she'd be there as soon as she decided what to wear, so I'm thinking October. Fashion is Natalie's life. I had a nightmare once—no kidding—in which Nat betrayed me to Pontius Pilate for thirty pieces of silver lamé fabric and the name of the hottest clothing designer in Jerusalem. (It was Easter time, what can I say?) I know, of course, that in real life she'd never do this. In real life she finds silver lamé exceedingly tacky.

Pat says, "Coke?"

I nod, and he goes over to the counter to get it.

I sit down across from Frankie, who smiles at me for a long minute, as if he can tell my shirt buttons have recently been undone. Worse thought: maybe they still are! I check this as discreetly as I can and determine that both buttons are secure; I sigh.

"Are you coming to the party?" he says, finally.

I say, "Most likely," and look beyond him to the front door.

Curtis Piperfield is walking in, without Bridget. They've got one of those weird relationships no one can figure out. They have broken up about twelve thousand times, and each time Curtis has done something desperately stupid, like spray-paint Bridget's name in huge letters across his garage door, or call me for a date.

Frankie is saying, "Has Natalie said anything?"

"Natalie says a lot of things," I tell him. "You'll have to be more specific." I know what he's getting at; I just want to make him say it.

"Anything about me?" He stares at his soda.

I throw him a bone: "She said you've got good posture."

"Yeah?" Frankie is thrilled. "She said that?"

"Once."

"Did she say anything else?"

"Like what?"

"Like anything."

"Like, if she likes you?"

"Whatever."

I could tell him that Natalie is nuts about him and make his summer. She *is* nuts about him, but that's not the point. The point is, I can't take it upon myself to tell Frankie Bruno that Natalie likes him until Natalie actually instructs me to tell Frankie that she told me she likes him.

"Do you want me to ask her if she likes you?"

Frankie shrugs. "If it happens to come up . . ."

Pat appears with the Cokes and slides into the booth. "Curtis and Bridget broke up," he tells us.

Frankie and I say, "Again?"

I check Pat's expression to see if he feels this development is cause for concern. He was pretty furious the last time Curtis and Bridget broke up for five minutes and Curtis called me. Patrick even sent a message to Curtis through Cluck.

C.C. is taken—that was the message.

As if I hadn't said the same thing to Curtis myself? (Actually, I told him I was *involved,* not *taken.* I figured Patrick was upset and not thinking straight, thus his poor word choice.) Not that I minded talking to Curtis on the phone. What I minded was Patrick minding that I'd talked to Curtis on the phone. I said as much to Cluck, who explained that as my official boyfriend Patrick had no choice. When I dismissed that as idiotic, Cluck told me, "It's a guy thing," which is his explanation for everything.

Then the cheerleaders and the would-be cheerleaders giggle into the burger place, and all the boys (except Patrick O'Connell) turn around to look at them. I notice that Kelly Sinclair passes awfully close to Cluck. That's Kelly—never say die. I have this mental image of her at home in her peach-colored bedroom, throwing darts at a photo of Grace, chanting, "That's all right, that's okay, we're gonna beat 'em anyway!" (If you knew Kelly, you would not think this was even remotely far-fetched.)

Grace throws her arms around Cluck and kisses him, right there in front of everybody.

Pat and I look at each other and laugh; it's an

inside joke. I don't mind saying that I love having an inside joke with Patrick. It makes me feel as if everyone else at the burger place is invisible. The joke is about the way Grace and Cluck are always kissing in public. For Pat and me, hand-holding and cheek-kissing is the limit—in public, that is. But Grace and Cluck have become quite the show-offs lately.

It occurs to me that Grace wanting to be a cheerleader may, in fact, be a logical extension of this need to show off—or vice versa.

One of the Simon Pete's preppies yells, "Get a room." Everyone laughs, but Grace and Cluck keep kissing. I notice that Kelly Sinclair is very pur-posefully looking somewhere else, which (as much as I hate to be in sync with Kelly) is what I usually do. But today, I don't, and I notice something that makes me shiver.

Cluck is kissing Grace, but he's looking at me! His eyes are open and he's staring across the burg-er place, and there's no question that he is staring at *me*. It's fast, though; if I'd been drinking my soda, I'd have missed it. The next moment, Cluck's eyes are closed, which, as any high school kid can tell you, is universally considered proper kissing form. But I am shivering nonetheless, and I wonder how many times before this I *was* drinking my soda when . . .

Pat gives my hand a gentle squeeze. "Maybe Friday."

For some reason, Friday is the farthest thing from my mind.

* * *

As dreams go, it's a quick one: St. Bernadette's gym is the setting again, but this time I have an aerial view. This is because I am on top of a human pyramid. The humans, of course, are the St. Simon Pete's cheerleaders, and I have to admit it's a pretty impressive structure—eighty, maybe ninety teenage girls high.

I am standing on Grace Boccaluzzo's shoulders. Kelly and Lisa are directly beneath her. Pat is there. Cluck is there. My mom is there, and she's pointing up at me and yelling something I can't hear. So I lean forward, and this gets Grace wobbling, which, as you might imagine, gets Kelly and Lisa and the other eighty or ninety girls wobbling as well.

Mom is still yelling something, but I still can't make it out. Patrick is yelling, too; he's yelling, "Maybe Friday." And Cluck's just standing there.

Grace and the others are wobbling like crazy. I lean even farther forward because I think I finally understand what my mother is saying. She is saying, "C.C., button your shirt!"

I check my buttons; two are undone. And then . . . I'm falling.

The other eighty or ninety cheerleaders are giggling, my mother is still yelling "Button your shirt . . . your shirt . . . your shirt . . ." and I'm falling. The fall is slow and fast at the same time. But when I land, it's not on the hard wood of the gym floor, it's in the soft security of someone's arms.

I'm about to thank Patrick for catching me, since, naturally, I assume he's the someone in whose arms I've landed. But when I look up, I see that it's not Patrick. Patrick and Mom and the cheerleaders are melting away into dream fog.

The someone is Cluck.

Chapter 3

I sit up in bed. My heart is beating fast and I'm sweating. I'm glad to be awake and out of the dream. My only regret is that I didn't stay in it long enough to ask Cluck why he was looking at me while he was kissing Grace.

I grab my journal from the nightstand and record the dream. Then I go back to sleep. The next thing I know it's Saturday morning and Natalie is barging through my bedroom door.

Nat is petite, with very delicate features, and since her mom finally gave in and let her get highlights, her hair is now this lush dark blond with golden flecks that make her brown eyes look even browner.

Today she is wearing cut-off shorts and a football jersey. She spins to show me the name printed across the back, and I see that this is the shirt she charmed off of Gordy Butterworth. The shirt is huge on her; the B and the H land almost at her elbows. I can tell it's making her feel especially cute. Which she is.

Natalie has become something of a hot commodity around Miltondale lately, and she has a whole collection of T-shirts, sweatshirts, and jerseys she's talked various boys into parting with. Personally, I think this is a useful and logical way of channeling her obsession with clothes.

Frankie Bruno will not be the least bit happy to see Nat in this jersey, which, I figure, is probably the whole point. Nat doesn't like Gordy like she likes Frankie, but she has told Frankie on numerous occasions that she doesn't want to be tied down. It drives Frankie crazy, which, again, is most likely the point.

Today we are going swimming at Salvatore Malanconico's house. Not just Nat and me—Nat and me and Pat and Frankie and Cluck and Grace (*after* cheerleading) along with some other Preppies and Bernie girls, plus a few kids from Miltondale Junior High just to make it interesting. Sal's pool should be able to handle it. Cluck says it's Olympic-sized.

Nat drops onto the bed beside me. "Is Grace coming?" she asks.

I slide out of bed and start rummaging through my drawers for a bathing suit. "She's going to meet us there," I say with very little enthusiasm, then hold up two suits. "One-piece, or bikini?"

Natalie winces. "Say *maillot,* C.C. Not one-piece."

I have never understood why Natalie finds certain fashion terms offensive. "Sorry. Which one?"

She jerks the jersey up to remind me that *she* is wearing a maillot today. This is my answer. I have been assigned bikini detail. According to Nat, it would be completely inappropriate for us to show up at Sal Malanconico's pool party together, wearing the same style bathing suit. I know better than to argue. But this will be my first public appearance in a bikini, so I'm a bit nervous.

Natalie goes to the kitchen to wait for me. I go into the bathroom and turn on the shower. While the water is getting hot, I dig through the vanity drawer for a new razor. That's probably the biggest lifestyle change I've undergone since having an actual boyfriend—I am now an excessively conscientious shaver. In the summer, you can always tell which girls aren't going out with anyone; they're stubbly.

I am in and out of the shower in exactly six minutes. I put on the bikini and throw my journal and a towel into a canvas bag. Then I grab a pair of shorts and head for the kitchen, where I find Natalie drinking tomato juice with my parents.

The first thing my father says is, "Change your bathing suit."

"Why?"

"Because you are not going out of the house like that."

"Like what?"

"Like *that.*"

This is typical of the conversations Dad and I have been having lately. Pointless, angry, diametrically opposed. And sometimes, like now, there's this tone in my father's voice. If I had to identify it, the best I could do is *scared.*

"Dad . . ."

"C.C. . . ."

"Mom! . . ." But Mom just sips her coffee. This is a land mine, and she's not touching it.

"You're not going out of the house like that," my father says again. "Put on a one-piece."

(Natalie is dying to correct him, I know it.) I turn around and stomp back to my room. Nat follows me.

"This will completely destroy our fashion agenda," she tells me. "Mother of God, C.C. You look great in that bikini."

"I think that's the problem." I pull the maillot out of the drawer a second time.

Nat sighs. "Is this a Catholic thing?"

I don't answer. It might be. Then an idea hits me, fast, like a poem. I put the maillot on over my bikini and slip on my shorts and the Prep swimming T-shirt Patrick gave me over that.

"You'd be a natural in public school, Cecily Carruthers," Nat tells me, which is the kind of compliment I get from Nat on a regular basis—the kind that has me wondering if I should go straight to confession.

As we get ready to leave, my dad stops us and asks if I put on my one-piece suit. He doesn't ask if I *changed* my suit, so I'm able to look him straight in the eye and say, "Yes."

He volunteers to drive us to Sal's house, which is nice of him, but my stomach hurts and I can't help wondering exactly when he and I started treating each other like enemies.

* * *

We get out of the car in front of Sal's house, and my father tells us to be careful and remember to thank Mrs. Malanconico when we leave.

I'm thinking, What am I, four? but I don't say it.

We walk around to the back. Frankie and Patrick

33

are sitting in patio chairs at the far end of the pool. There are five girls seated in Patrick's immediate vicinity (no accident, believe me). We do a quick count: three bikinis, two maillots.

One of the girls is Lisa Bruno (maillot); another is her cheerleader friend Monica Baylor (bikini). I don't recognize the rest but Nat does. She says they all go to Miltondale Junior High and are marginally important there. She also says that Lisa should have chosen a suit that drew attention away from her big rear end.

I ask Sal if I can use the bathroom. He says, sure, go ahead, so Nat waits for me on the patio, and I go in through the kitchen. Mrs. Malanconico is sitting at the table drinking tea. She has very expensive-looking fingernails. She smiles, so I introduce myself.

"C.C.?" Now she's really smiling. "Aren't you the girl Sal's had a crush on for so long?"

Am I? I mean, it wouldn't be unheard of. But since I have no hard evidence, I just shrug. How did she expect me to answer that question anyway? And, more to the point, why would a boy's mother *ever* bring that up?

She directs me to the "powder room." Inside, I remove my T-shirt, shorts, and one layer of swimwear. I stuff the clothes into my bag. Then, even though Nat says I look great in the bikini, I intentionally drape my towel around myself so that I look as if I *haven't* intentionally draped my towel around myself.

Back through the kitchen—I thank Mrs. Malanconico—and go out to the patio. I see that Nat is still wearing Gordy's jersey, and I know this is because she wants to be certain Frankie sees it.

Pat notices me and waves me over; I could jump him on the spot, but I don't. Lisa Bruno notices me, too, and I can tell she is embarrassed to be caught hanging around my boyfriend again. Ha. Good.

I say, "Hi, Lisa."

"Hi, C.C."

"Hi, Monica."

"Hi, C.C."

Teenage small talk. Mindless but necessary. Not saying hi, even to someone you can't stand, is grounds for vicious gossip and possible exile. Natalie says her hi's, then removes the jersey.

Monica says, "I like your suit."

Lisa is inching her big behind over on her towel so that she is now five or six inches farther away from Patrick than she was to begin with. This is done either out of respect for me, or because there's a pebble under her towel. I don't care; five inches is five inches.

Then the Miltondale girls say hi to Natalie and sort of wave to me, so I say hi to them even though I have no idea who any of them are. I wish I were better at math because I would really like to know how many of these compulsory hi's have been exchanged. I figure the combinations are infinite . . . C.C. to Lisa, C.C. to Monica, Monica and Lisa to C.C., Monica and Lisa to Natalie, Natalie to Lisa, Miltondale girl #1 to Natalie . . . and so on. It's ten minutes into summer vacation and already I'm socially exhausted.

"I thought there was cheerleading practice," I say to Lisa.

"There was. It's over."

This shouldn't surprise me; after all, how long does it take to learn how to jump up and down and scream your head off? "Where's Grace?" I ask.

Lisa shrugs; clearly, since Grace is not yet a cheerleader—and since it remains to be seen whether or not she ever will, in fact, *be* a cheerleader—it is presently not Lisa's responsibility to know, or care, where she is.

Pat has left his patio chair to stand beside me. "You look great," he says.

This gives me the courage to remove the intentionally draped towel. I say, "So do you."

And he does. Patrick O'Connell is a human triangle—broad shoulders leading to a slender waist, with a stomach that ripples in between. His crucifix, as always, rests in the chasm between his incredible pecs. I like that word—*chasm.* It's got a strong, masculine undertone that seems appropriate for describing a body like Patrick's. It's a nice contrast to Patrick's innate gentleness. It's poetry.

Pat gives me a small kiss, and the Miltondale girls look as if they're about to explode. I can feel the envy, like the heat rising from the cement, and it makes me nervous. Some girls—Kelly, for example—might not mind it. But in my opinion, with envy comes a great deal of risk.

Pat tells me he's going to swim laps. I spread out my towel and (along with the other females) watch him for a minute or so. Then I take my journal out of the canvas bag and roll over onto my stomach to start a poem. It's a poem I've been needing to write, about my dad. I feel a little weird that this will be the first poem I don't get to show Sister Jude right away, or ever, since she's now connected to the cheerleaders. Nat is shading her eyes, saying, "Look at Frankie on the diving board."

But I am remembering my father's voice and have already lost myself in the poem.

* * *

Natalie practically has to slug me to get me out of the poem. Getting slugged out of a poem is a little like having someone wake you from a deep sleep with a police siren.

Natalie points to Grace, who is sitting nearby, crying her eyes out. I didn't even know she'd arrived.

"What's wrong?" I ask Grace.

And Grace answers, "Nothing."

I hate it when people do that, and Grace does it a lot. She's also famous for saying her hair looks crummy when she knows it looks perfect, and for telling people how fat she is just to hear them tell her she isn't. I look at Natalie, who shrugs. So I say, "Are you sure, Grace?"

Grace nods. "I'm sure."

This is Grace's way of getting attention. So here I go: "C'mon, Grace . . ."

"I'm fine. Really."

What does she think I am, an idiot? I'm starting to get annoyed. Not because she's upset, but because she's telling me she isn't upset when she's clearly extremely upset.

The Miltondale girls are staring, and Lisa and Monica are ready to burst because they know there is only one thing that can make a girl cry like that—two, if you include getting your hand slammed in a car door. But I know, in this case, it's not a car door, it's the other thing.

"What did Cluck do?"

Grace wipes her eyes.

"Tell us, Grace," says Natalie, who's studying Grace's bathing suit. She probably wants to get past this trauma so she can ask Grace where she bought it.

Grace takes a deep breath. She hesitates, as if she's trying to decide what to say. Then she finally blurts out, "He wants to see other people."

Natalie says, "Anyone in particular?" and I give her an elbow to the ribs. Too late. Grace is hysterical again.

"It'll be all right," I say.

"You can do better," says Nat. It's standard dialogue for the situation, but totally inaccurate. Aside from Patrick, Cluck is as good as it gets. My guess is that Lisa, Monica, and the Miltondale girls are already plotting to murder each other just to improve their own odds with him.

Grace calms down a bit. "Ya think?"

"Sure," I say. But I have this feeling she's not telling me everything. If she were Nat, I'd be able to guess exactly what she wasn't telling me. Then again, if she were Nat she *would* be telling me everything. I'm about to ask Grace what really happened, but Natalie can no longer control herself.

"Did you get that suit at Braddock's?" she asks. This distracts Grace, which, as it turns out, is a good thing, because she doesn't see what I see: good old Cluck arriving fashionably late at Sal Malanconico's pool party.

With Kelly Sinclair.

Chapter 4

My first instinct is to throw Kelly and Cluck into the deep end and hope they both drown. Talk about a guy thing! This is the guy thing to end all guy things.

Everyone except Grace, who's crying again, has turned to watch Cluck and Kelly as they come through the gate into the pool area.

Natalie mouths, "You tell her."

And I lip back, "No way. You tell her."

Then one of the Miltondale girls says, "Cluck came with that cheerleader." (Kelly is often referred to as *that* cheerleader as opposed to merely *a* cheerleader—*that* cheerleader being a title of sorts.)

Grace stops crying so suddenly, I'm afraid she's dead. She looks, and—there's no denying it—

Cluck and *that* cheerleader have indeed arrived simultaneously.

Natalie shades her eyes to get a better look at Kelly across the pool. "Her suit is from last season," she informs us, as if that's supposed to help.

Grace says, "What should I do?"

My suggestion is, "Nothing."

Even Lisa Bruno, who has been known to sleep over at Kelly's on occasion, pipes up and agrees with me. "Pretend it doesn't bother you," she advises Grace.

Who asked her? I narrow my eyes at Lisa. "It does bother her."

"I know it bothers her, but she doesn't want them to know it bothers her."

"I think you're bothering her," says Nat.

Lisa gives her a wicked look. I'm sure Nat could care less.

Grace has not moved. Secretly, I'm glad, because if she decides to get up and leave the party, I'll have to go with her (she's not a cheerleader *yet*). I'm not exactly thrilled at the thought of leaving Patrick here with Lisa Bruno and the Miltondale girls, not to mention Monica Baylor, who most definitely does not have a big rear end.

Patrick comes splashing across the pool and hoists himself out to sit on the edge.

"Wow," he says.

"That's one word for it," I say. I hand him a towel. "Does he *like* her?" I am asking, of course, on Grace's behalf. But for some reason, I sound a little panicked. (It is turning out to be a very complicated day, and we haven't even reached peak tanning hours yet.)

Pat does not answer, and this is because Cluck and Kelly are approaching us. To me, they don't look especially *together,* but this may be a trick of the light. I've got to give Grace credit, she holds her head up and does not attempt to impale Kelly on the pole of one of Mrs. Malanconico's patio umbrellas.

Cluck looks at Patrick. "Yow."

Pat gives him a wave, then slips back into the pool and resumes his laps.

"It's hot as hell," remarks Cluck, almost to Grace.

Out of habit, I say, "Don't cuss."

Grace gets up and goes into the Malanconicos' house, and I can just picture Sal's mother at the kitchen table asking her, "Aren't you the girl Gilbert McNally just humiliated in front of everyone?"

Nat looks at Kelly and says, "I used to have that suit."

Kelly smiles. The idiot thinks it's a compliment. Nat rolls her eyes.

I myself am not looking at Kelly, I'm looking at Cluck, who actually has the gall to say, "Hi, babe."

To which I have no reply. Cluck has not used that phrase since I started dating Pat and he started (and, if you want to get technical, finished) dating Grace.

But he says it, right in front of Kelly Sinclair: Hi, babe.

Kelly, perhaps having once been advised by Lisa Bruno, acts as if it doesn't bother her. But I know it bothers her. The thing I can't understand is why, for the first time in eleven years, it doesn't bother me.

Now there's this very awkward silence, which Frankie Bruno sees as his opportunity to start throwing the girls in the water. As far as I'm concerned, his timing couldn't be better. I mean, where were we supposed to go from Hi, babe?

Frankie scoops up Natalie and dumps her into the pool. Sal runs by and gives Kelly a nice hard shove that knocks her in, and the Miltondale boys start grabbing the Miltondale girls. There is laughter and some halfhearted protesting. Everyone is screaming. Lisa and Monica get up and run. Nobody chases them. (Ha.) They jump in on their own, which, I don't have to tell you, is utterly pathetic.

Now everyone is in the pool but me and Cluck.

I say, "You should throw me in." For appearances, naturally.

"We're beyond that," he tells me.

I notice that his nose and cheekbones are beginning to sunburn, which makes his eyes, which are usually dusty blue like mine, look even more vivid than usual. There is also a glimmer of hurt in his eyes. He's looking at me, and I'm looking at him and remembering about nine trillion things we've done together.

"Why are you with her?" I demand, but I'm more curious than angry and this is because I've never known Cluck to do anything really mean. "Why did you come with her?"

Cluck's jaw is set. "I didn't."

"Cluck. I saw you."

"You saw *me*," he says. "And you saw *her.*" There is more to say, but I don't think he's planning to say it.

Cluck drags his hand through his hair. Nobody else has hair like Cluck's, at least nobody *I* know.

If you look closely, you can see that almost every strand is a different shade of brown. (Nat swears he highlights; I know better.) When Cluck is very still, which is practically never, his hair looks as if it were carved from cherrywood.

"Do you like Kelly?" I ask him. "This time."

"It's hard to explain," says Cluck. "She's Kelly."

I say, "It's a guy thing."

And he smiles.

I look for Patrick in the pool. One of the Miltondale girls is splashing him. This is my cue. I get up and dive in, leaving Cluck alone—which, I have a feeling, is exactly what he's come to expect from me.

I swim over to Patrick and he puts his arms around me. He is bare-chested; I've got about two ounces of Lycra Spandex covering my boobs. So far, this is as close to naked as we've ever been in each other's company. He is about to say something, when Frankie Bruno does a cannonball off the diving board. The splash sends a wave rolling over our heads.

We go under.

And that's when I feel Patrick's hand land on my breast. Two seconds later, we are back above the surface.

"That was an accident," he says, breathing.

"It's okay."

"I'm sorry."

"It's okay."

"Are you sure?"

I nod, pushing my hair back. It's okay, because I know beyond any doubt that Patrick O'Connell would never intentionally do anything as tawdry as copping a feel in broad daylight in front of everybody we know. Even so, I'm trembling.

Pat puts his arms around me again. "That didn't count, did it?" he asks.

I hope not. I'd hate to have to remember getting to second base this way, in a swimming pool full of cheerleaders, no less! Also, I'm not an expert, but I think for it to count there's probably some kind of time requirement. So I tell Patrick, "No. That didn't count."

"Good."

Now Mrs. Malanconico appears from the kitchen with iced tea and sodas. Grace is with her, carrying paper cups and a couple thousand bags of chips.

Everyone starts climbing out of the pool and drying off, but Pat seems reluctant to let go of me. I don't mind exactly, but I am a little thirsty.

"Hey . . ." He looks nervous.

"What?"

"I want to tell you something," Patrick says in a very silky voice. He gives me this crooked kind of not-quite-a-smile, and I'm not sure, but I get the distinct feeling that he's reasoning with himself— as if there's a little voice in his head coaxing him or reminding him that it's time for something.

So I do a little coaxing of my own. I sprinkle a few small kisses on his cheekbone.

Pat squirms thankfully. He's ready to crack. . . .

But then Sal is calling Patrick for a volleyball game, so Pat pulls me even closer and says something really fast—so fast that I'm not even sure if he said what I think he said.

He lets go of me and swims away, and when he climbs up the ladder, I say, "Excuse me?"

And Patrick O'Connell, who looks just as perfect dripping wet as he does completely dry, turns around and says, right out loud in front of everybody, "I said, I love you."

* * *

Mrs. O'Connell gives us a ride home. Patrick is in front; Nat, Grace, and I are in back. I can see Mrs. O'Connell's eyes in the rearview mirror, and I can tell she thinks it is the most adorable thing in the world that her son has a girlfriend. Mrs. O'Connell is that type—she's got four boys (Pat is the oldest), and I figure any day now she's going to invite me to go shopping or out to lunch. I'd like to know what portion of her life is spent putting down the toilet seat.

She asks us how the party was, and it's all I can do to keep from shouting, "Patrick said he loves me!" at the top of my lungs.

Grace is moping.

Natalie says, "I like your blouse, Mrs. O'Connell."

And Mrs. O'Connell says, "Thank you, Natalie. I got it at Braddock's."

They have bonded for life.

Pat throws me this look over his shoulder. It's a sweet, private look—the kind you only see boys giving to girls they love. I used to get it from Cluck a lot, but I pretended not to notice.

Now Mrs. O'Connell is telling me how excited she is that Pat's little brother, Mikey, is going to be in my mother's kindergarten class next year, and suddenly I'm wondering about the first time Mrs. O'Connell let Mr. O'Connell go to second.

This throws me. What am I, some kind of pervert? Why would I wonder something like that? I'm probably blushing like crazy. This is a thoroughly inappropriate thought. Fascinating, but inappropriate.

Mrs. O'Connell drops us off at my house; Pat is dying to kiss me, I know, but his mom is sitting right there in the driver's seat, so it's not a possibility. I was even a little uncomfortable having Mrs. Malanconico see us in the pool with our arms around each other. In spite of this picture of a teenage Mr. O'Connell pawing a teenage Mrs. O'Connell that's stuck in my head, I am a person with great regard for privacy.

"Come for dinner one night, C.C.," Mrs. O'Connell says.

I say sure, and thank her for the ride. Grace manages a mopey thank you and Nat says, "Thank you, Mrs. O'Connell. Maybe I'll see you at Braddock's." She's got pretty good manners, for a public-school kid.

Pat says he'll call me tomorrow—he has to baby-sit Mikey tonight.

We go inside. I really want to tell Nat and Grace what happened in the pool, but Grace's Cluck trauma has the right of way and we all know it.

Grace opens with, "I can't believe he showed up with Kelly."

"That was cold," Nat agrees.

"He knew I was going to be there," Grace wails. "And he came with her."

"Tell us about the breakup," says Nat.

"There's nothing to tell," says Grace, which, you've got to admit, is ridiculous. Also, there is this weird look on her face that I can't help thinking is guilt.

"Maybe he didn't come with her," I say.

"C.C.!" Nat stares at me. "We saw them."

I shake my head. "We saw him. And we saw her."

"Which means? . . ."

"I don't know. Maybe they just happened to get there at the same time. Maybe they just walked in together." After all, it would be just like Kelly to stick herself to Cluck on the way in, knowing we'd all assume she was his date. (And it would be just like Cluck to trust me to understand that this was what had happened.)

Suddenly, I feel crummy about not giving Cluck the benefit of the doubt right from the start.

"Maybe," says Grace, but she's still sniffling.

My turn. "Guess what?" I say.

They both say, "What?" (Grace's what, of course, is mopey.)

I hesitate a moment, because I don't exactly know

how to tell them that Pat and I had an accidental brush with second base. Even though Grace is (or was) a flagrant kisser, and Natalie goes to public school, I'm not sure what they're going to think.

I open the fridge and grab Cokes for Grace and me and a diet root beer for Natalie.

"In the pool today, Patrick . . . his hand . . . it was on my . . ."

Grace and Nat take their sodas. Grace is now more interested than mopey. "On your what, C.C.?" she asks.

"You know." I shrug, then kind of motion to my chest area with my chin. "You know." They're looking at me as if I'm some kind of imbecile. So to clarify, I say, "It was like second. Almost." Then, in case they didn't get it, I say, "Second *base.*"

Only now does it occur to me what a completely stupid metaphor that is. What does a boy touching your boobs have to do with baseball? Nothing.

I don't get a chance to comment on this, however, because suddenly Grace and Natalie are laughing. Actually, Natalie is laughing—Grace is giggling.

Nat says, "So?"

Which strikes me as pretty insensitive. What does she mean, so? Isn't the first one of us getting to second, even almost to second, a singularly significant event? Unless . . .

I look at Grace. For some reason, I feel like a stranger in my own kitchen. "Have you and Cluck? . . ."

Grace nods.

I turn to Nat. "You and Frankie? . . ."

A nod from Nat.

I don't mind saying that this totally floors me. My two best friends (three, if you include Cluck, which, I suppose, you'd have to) have already gotten to second base! And they never even told me. Why?

"Why didn't you tell me?"

"Because we know how you are," says Nat.

"How am I?"

"You know," says Grace.

"I don't know."

"We thought it would bother you," Grace says. "Because of how you are."

"Why would it bother *me?*" I demand. It does bother me a little, but, if we've learned anything at all from Lisa Bruno, it's to not let anyone know. "They're *your* stupid boobs! And what does that mean, 'because of how you are.' How am I?"

"Catholic," says Nat.

"Grace is Catholic," I remind her.

"You're better at it," says Grace.

"C.C., really," says Nat. "It's just one base away from kissing."

See how ridiculous that sounds? I sink into a kitchen chair and take a long swallow of Coke. I am, more or less, in shock. I hear myself saying, "Are you still virgins?"

Nat answers immediately: "Yes."

Grace is slower off the block. "Mostly."

"Mostly?" I am so Catholic that I don't even know what she means. But what I am beginning to understand is that, apparently, I'm way behind schedule.

"Don't feel bad," Grace says. "You were the first one to get Frenched."

"Frenched sounds disgusting," I tell her. "French *kissed*."

"Grace is right." Nat sits down beside me. "You hit the ground running, C.C."

This is small consolation. I wonder if Pat is as naive as I am about the sexuality running rampant around us. This certainly puts a whole new spin on Lisa Bruno's party.

We drink our sodas quietly for a minute. I'm aching to ask Grace if she went to confession. I'm aching to ask thirty-four zillion other questions, too, not the least of which is, "What was it like?"

"Okay," says Nat.

"Excellent," says Grace.

I assume the difference has to do with Frankie and Cluck.

Nat says she's willing to provide me with additional information should I need any. But she doesn't push the issue, this, I imagine, being due to How I Am.

"So is it just you two?" I ask. "Or is it everybody? Lisa, Monica, Kelly . . ."

"Everybody," Nat assures me.

"Lisa and Monica are going to be *seniors,*" Grace says.

I'm thinking: what, second base is like geometry—you've got to get it over with by sophomore year? I hear the phrase "it's time" echo in my brain; where'd *that* come from?

Grace says she thinks, as far as second is concerned, everybody pretty much hit their stride sometime in the middle of May. It's old news. This kills me.

Sexually speaking, I am an underachiever.

I promise myself that next Friday I'm going to second.

Chapter 5 ─────────

My mother wakes me up early the following morning, which is not entirely to my liking, since I was up late working on the poem I started at Frankie's. She has a suggestion.

"Why don't you help Daddy in the yard?"

I have not helped my father in the yard since the fifth grade. We laughed a lot then, but of course the phrase "you're not going out of the house like that" didn't come up much.

I say, "What about Mass?"

"After Mass," she says.

"I'll think about it."

We go to the eight o'clock service, as usual. I see Kelly there, and I have this crazy image of her getting up at the lector's podium and making an announcement to the parish regarding cheerleading tryouts next week. She would, too, if they'd let her.

Kelly is with her older brother, Tim, who just graduated from Simon Pete's and is extremely good-looking. Tim was a hoops sensation at Prep his junior year; then he threw the entire athletic department into a tailspin by opting to spend his senior year abroad. Cluck told me that Tim blew his scholarship and his eligibility. I don't know— he looks pretty darn eligible to me.

Personally, I think Tim Sinclair made the right choice; those nine months in Europe really show. He looks rested, not to mention sexy, and European sexy is different from American sexy. It's smarter, edgier. I'm sure Patrick would vehemently object to me looking at Tim so intently, but I don't feel I'm doing anything wrong. I haven't seen Tim in a while, so I'm not flirting exactly, I'm just sort of catching up. I picture him dribbling around Europe—up and down the Spanish Steps, along the Champs-Élysées.

It's very hot in church. The transoms beneath the stained-glass windows are all open, which results in several of the saints missing their feet. There are two fans on the altar, which ruin the acoustics for the choir when they sing the Hosannas.

My parents and I go up to the altar to receive

Communion, and on the way back I *happen* to glance toward Tim Sinclair. He has just returned to his seat, where he should be bowing his head to give thanks for the Blessed Sacrament. But he's not bowing his head, he's watching me. He watches me all the way up the outer aisle and even turns his head a little when I pass. This, I don't mind saying, shoots a thrill right through me; I only hope it does-n't counteract the effect of the Eucharist.

Then Mass is ended and I go in peace to serve God . . . and, believe it or not, to get hit on by Tim Sinclair.

He says, "Hi."

I'm waiting on the sidewalk. Dad has gone for the car and Mom is still inside, signing up for some bake sale. I say, "Hi."

"Cecily Carruthers, right?"

I say, "Yes."

"How are you?"

"Fine. You?"

"Great."

"How was Europe?"

"Great."

It's weird to see Tim wearing anything other than his Prep basketball uniform. Sister Jude in freshman English would call it taking him "out of context." Oddly enough, though, Tim doesn't look out of anything. He looks . . . well, I don't know . . . *comfortable.* Extra comfortable. Maybe it's merely the effect of recently receiving the Body of Christ. Maybe it's not.

Tim expounds a little on his answer to my Europe question. This is now beginning to feel less like being hit on and more like having a conversation. I don't mind, actually. He seems wildly impressed by the fact that I pronounce Michelangelo correctly. What did he think I was, an airhead or something? It occurs to me that he probably did. I smile at Tim. He smiles back.

Dad pulls up with the car just as my mother comes down the steps. I brace myself to make introductions. (Please, God, don't let Mom invite Tim to Come for Dinner One Night.) But Tim is leaving. "I'll see you around," he says, and I say, "Sure. See you around," and he says, "Yeah, I hope so," which gives me another smug feeling because I can tell he means it.

* * *

The first thing I do when I get home is call Nat and tell her Tim Sinclair said see you around and meant it.

Nat laughs, then says, "Come over."

"I can't. I have to help my father in the yard." Before she can ask, I say, "It's not a Catholic thing. It's a yard thing."

Nat says she might be meeting Frankie later at the burger place, so I say maybe I'll see her there. I hang up and go change into shorts and a T-shirt, and find my father out front. It's four thousand degrees.

"Where should I start?"

He looks a little apprehensive, as if maybe he doesn't trust me with the lawn mower It *has* been five years since we've done this.

"Dad?"

He points to the flowers along the walkway. "You can weed those, I guess."

The next thing I know, I'm wearing beat-up canvas gloves and kneeling in topsoil. Dad is clipping spent blooms from the rosebush.

"Who was that boy you were talking to after Mass?"

"Tim."

"Tim who?"

"Tim Sinclair."

"He goes to Prep?"

I shake my head. "Just graduated. He's going to college."

"College?" Dad accidentally lops off a perfectly good rose.

"One of the Jesuit ones. I forget which."

"Are you planning to go out with him?"

"Go out with him? No."

"He's starting college."

"I know he's starting college!" *I* told *him* that.

Dad says, "What about Patrick?"

"What *about* Patrick?" I ask.

"What about you and Patrick?"

"I don't understand the question."

Dad puts down the clippers. "Don't," he tells me.

I stop weeding. "Don't what?"

"Don't anything." He clears his throat. "Just . . . don't."

For a moment, I think the heat is getting to him. Then I realize that this is my father talking to me about sex. Mother of God! I'm going to curl up and die. Really, I am.

It gets quiet; I'm weeding like a madwoman now.

Dad has picked up the clippers and he's chopping the singed roses off the bush with new resolve. They fall, like ruined cake decorations, and I almost cry. Because it occurs to me that the problem isn't that Dad doesn't trust me with the lawn mower.

The problem is that Dad doesn't trust me.

* * *

This is one of those rare occasions when I enter the burger place alone; ordinarily, I'm with Pat or Natalie or Grace and Cluck. Sunday is a slow day at the burger place—mostly there are families with little kids. Once Pat and I brought Mikey for a milkshake; he whined the whole time, then accidentally dumped the shake in Pat's lap. Never again, I swore it.

I look around and see Natalie and Frankie sitting in a booth. I head there, trying to make myself forget that they've already gotten to second base, which I still can't believe. For all I know, they've gone even further than that. I feel very inexperienced and a little uncomfortable.

There's this other feeling, too—it's the same feeling I had yesterday when I realized that Sister Jude is now a member of the opposition (cheerleaders), and that I probably wouldn't be sharing my poetry with her any more. I feel lonely.

"Hi, C.C."

"Hi, Nat. Hi, Frankie." I take a seat across from Nat, beside Frankie.

I see that Natalie is finally wearing something of Frankie's—a T-shirt with the name and logo of his father's gas station printed across the front. Across her chest, to be exact, and what do you think that brings to my mind?

They've been having their usual discussion, I can tell. Nat has been saying she doesn't want to be tied down, she likes things the way they are, and Frankie's trying not to sound obsessed, but he's been begging her to make their relationship more serious. I happen to know that a development of this sort would cut Natalie's T-shirt wardrobe by eighty percent.

Then Nat's eyes go round and she says, "Look who's here."

I'm hoping Pat but figuring Cluck (with or without Kelly; it's a tossup). But when I turn around, it's not Pat or Cluck. It's Tim Sinclair. He stops at the counter for a soda, then spots us and smiles. If Grace were here, she'd say he looks "soooooo delicious," and I'd probably have to agree.

Then Tim Sinclair, who, in case you've forgotten, is going to be a freshman in *college,* sits down across from me, beside Nat.

"Hello, again."

I make the introductions. Frankie says he remembers watching Tim play basketball at Prep. I remember, too. Every female in Miltondale remembers. Tim is the Cluck of his graduating class. To be honest, it's a little bit scary having him sit here with me, but it's also exciting. He's wearing a T-shirt that I'm sure he bought in Europe. Natalie would kill for it, I know.

"Want a soda?" Tim asks me.

"Sure."

He goes to the counter and orders me a Coke. I wonder if he knows his sister hates me. I wonder if he would be buying me this soda if he knew that, until yesterday, I was completely misinformed regarding sexual expectations among my peer group.

Tim returns with my soda.

"Kelly tells me you go out with some guy from Prep," he says, handing me a straw.

I nod, but this doesn't send Tim running for the exit. He just smiles and says, "Lucky guy." He doesn't look as if he feels that buying me a Coke is out of line. Pat, on the other hand, would probably see things differently. Pat loves me, after all. So I suppose I should tell Tim Sinclair to get out of the booth and get lost. Then again, it's a free country.

I ask him if he had a girlfriend in Europe. My guess is he had twelve or thirteen thousand.

"I met a girl in Venice," Tim says. "But we decided to see other people for the summer."

Nat says, "Good plan."

Frankie gives her a sulky look.

Then guess who appears at our booth, carrying Mikey piggyback. Patrick. My boyfriend.

"Hi, C.C."

"Hi." I swallow hard, then I say, "Tim, this is Patrick. My boyfriend. Patrick, this is Tim Sinclair."

Mikey is going, "Milkshake! Milkshake!"

Tim gets up and shakes Pat's hand. Then he looks at me and says, "See you around."

Natalie is gripping her diet root beer, I assume to keep herself from jumping up and ripping the shirt off Tim's back.

No one says a word till Tim is out the door. Then Patrick puts Mikey in the booth, looks at me and says, "Can I talk to you for a second?"

Mikey is still screaming for his milkshake, so I get up and follow Pat to the counter where he orders a junior-size vanilla shake. He looks as if he's about to explode. Or cry.

"That was nothing," I say.

"It was something to me." Pat stares down at the counter. "It was you sitting in a booth with Tim Sinclair."

"He just sat," I tell Patrick. "I didn't ask him to sit."

"But you didn't ask him not to, did you?"

The last thing I need right now is a double negative.

The kid behind the counter slides the milkshake across to Pat. Pat takes a straw from the dispenser and stabs it through the whipped-cream topping. I probably should tell him I'm sorry, but the thing is, I'm not sorry. In my opinion, I have nothing to be sorry about. I mean, last I heard, Thou Shalt Not Sit with Other Boys wasn't a commandment. Anyway, wasn't he surrounded by girls when I got to Sal's party? Yes! And did I get crazy? No!

But he looks as lonely as I feel, so I lean close to him and, instead of "I'm sorry," I whisper, "I love you."

I hadn't meant to say that, but something told me it was what Pat was expecting. I've never been one for sticking to schedules, but just saying those words to Pat gives me a shimmery, electric feeling in my stomach. Clearly, this is a signal that I meant it, right? I happen to like the feeling of shimmering electricity, so I say it again.

"I love you."

Pat looks up from the milkshake. "What took you so long?" he asks. Then he gives me this soft, fast kiss on my lips. "I love you, too," he tells me.

But I already knew that.

* * *

I'm lying in bed, the way I used to when I'd listen to Curtis playing his guitar across the street. I never hear it anymore because, since Bridget, he's basically given up the guitar. Once in a while, I can hear him fighting with her on the phone, but it's not the same. I sort of miss the music, if you want to know the truth, and I think this has something to do with this weird loneliness I've been experiencing lately.

I'm writing in my journal about how it felt to tell Patrick I love him. I'm writing about how it felt to have Tim Sinclair flirting with me—not nearly as shimmery or electric, but still pretty good. Then I close the journal and think about Grace and Cluck, then about Kelly and Cluck, then just about Cluck, and how it used to seem so natural for him to climb through my window to play Truth or Dare with me and Natalie when she slept over on Friday nights. Of course, that was before Pat and I started going out.

I'm also thinking about being the last to get to second, as opposed to being the first to get French kissed. This is unsettling. Generally I am a trendsetter. But in this case, I guess, I am extra-Catholic. I'm sure my dad (whose advice, if you'll recall, was "Don't") would be very relieved to hear this. Still, I'd hate to think I'd reached my romantic peak at fourteen and a half!

I close my eyes and try to remember how it felt when Pat's hand slipped in the pool and wound up you-know-where for less than a millisecond. Not bad, but not exactly memorable, either. Of course, there were several thousand gallons of chlorinated water involved. I have no frame of reference, but I imagine that makes a difference. Also, neither of us was breathing oxygen at the time, and then there's always the buoyancy issue. My instincts tell me these combined factors should be taken into consideration.

Here's the problem: I don't know how second base is *supposed* to feel. Also, I just can't seem to get past this whole irrelevant baseball metaphor. So maybe I'm only falling behind because I'm not entirely comfortable with the terminology.

I reach for the phone and dial Cluck, figuring he's an expert. It's almost midnight, and I'm reminded that The Separate Phone Line is perhaps the single most significant advancement in inter-teenager communication since The Note Passed in Study Hall.

Cluck answers with a sleepy "Yow?"

"It's C.C."

"Hi, babe."

"Stop that."

"Hell of a time to call," he says.

"Don't cuss." I take a deep breath. "Okay, this isn't easy."

"Since when has anything about you been easy, C.C.?"

I don't think I like the inference. But I skip it and cut right to the chase. "Is there another term for second, other than second?"

"What the hell are you talking about?"

"Cluck!" I fall back into the pillows and sigh. "Second base."

"Since when are you interested in baseball?"

"I'm not. I'm talking about the other second base. The sex one."

I'm not surprised that this sends Cluck into hysterics. When he finally quits laughing I say, "Well. *Is* there another term for it?"

"You can say felt up, I guess. Why?"

"Just wondering."

"You plan on getting felt up, C.C.?"

(Tough question.) "Stop it."

"You started it."

(He's got a point.) "Are there any *other* choices?" I'm not exactly crazy about "felt up."

Cluck hesitates. "Groped. How does groped grab you?"

"It doesn't. What else you got?"

"Nothing."

"Oh. Well, thanks anyway."

"You're welcome. Night, babe."

"Good night."

The call leaves me feeling tangled up and restless. Clearly, I'm making too much of this. My perspective is off. As Natalie so eloquently put it: it's just one base away from kissing.

I roll over into my pillow and accidentally start thinking about something Grace said: that she was "mostly" a virgin. Okay, so what does that make Cluck? His voice, that "Night babe," is still cottony in my ear, and it doesn't make sense that Cluck could do something that important without . . .

Without what?

Without . . . *me?*

This thought sends me bolt upright in bed. I tell myself I didn't mean that the way it seemed, all I meant was . . . was that Cluck had some nerve, losing most of his virginity without *telling* me.

But then, he, more than anyone, knows How I Am.

Still, I was there when Cluck took the training wheels off his bike, and he was there the first time I swam underwater. We stole Milky Ways together once. Virginity—losing it, keeping it, doling it out in fractions—was simply never a variable in this equation we call our relationship. But now, Grace is claiming that she's given up at least a portion of hers (I'm still not clear on whether or not that's possible), and I can only assume that Cluck was on the receiving end.

I decide to get some sleep, because I have the feeling I'm going to be woken up early in the morning by a very good poem.

* * *

Tonight she discovers
how the cool sheet slips away,
and she collects him
to commit
what will remain there
in the heat.
Moths snow in the dark against their window;
it is a scene
not a moment.
He has forgotten her
already.

I read the poem twice before I realize it's not about Pat and me. A poem about us, at this point anyway, wouldn't involve sheets. I read it a third time and decide it's a little cynical. A scene is something played, or acted, as opposed to a moment, which is more sincere, more deeply felt.

I've got to admit, I like this poem. But I do feel kind of sorry for the couple, and I'm glad it's not us.

Chapter 6

When a poem gets you up early, there's just no going back to sleep. So by eight o'clock I'm dressed and out the door. I head for Natalie's house, but I take my time because there's a strange, summery silence to the neighborhood that's good for thinking. As I turn the corner I hear the sound of Cluck's garage door going up. When I look, he's standing there, framed by the wide rectangle of the bay. His arms are raised over his head, his hands clasped onto the door handle. He's wearing boxer shorts and nothing else; it's quite a picture, believe me. Every muscle in his upper body is defined, and his dark hair is all sweepy across his eyes.

"Yow," he says and gives me a sleepy grin.

I stop at the end of his driveway. "Trash day?"

He nods, lets go of the handle, and pushes his

arms outward in a wide stretch. If I weren't used to Cluck and his perfection, this might make my knees go weak. He grabs two barrels and drags them out to the curb. Then he takes my hand and tugs me toward the house. "Hungry?"

I shrug. "Sure. What's for breakfast?"

"Me."

"Funny." I follow him inside and tell him to put on some clothes. Then I go into the kitchen and wait for him. When he comes out one minute later, he's wearing jeans and a T-shirt (I am not disappointed. I'm *not!*)

"How many?" he asks.

"Two."

Scrambled eggs—Cluck's specialty. They're incredible. He uses milk and a lot of seasoning, but his secret is that he whisks them for one entire minute. (I got that secret out of him during one of our more innocent games of Truth or Dare, back in seventh grade.) The thing about these eggs is that they always manage to taste familiar, and at the same time like something I've never eaten before.

"Still thinking of getting felt up?" he asks, cracking an egg with one hand.

I don't answer. He's busy whisking anyway, and,

if you must know, I like to watch Cluck cook. It's the only time he doesn't look dangerous. Don't get me wrong—dangerous looks great on Cluck. But when Cluck is scrambling eggs, he's completely harmless. I can tell, from the way he's being extra quiet with the pan, that the rest of his family is still asleep.

"You didn't bring Kelly to Sal's," I say when he sets the plate in front of me. "Did you?"

Cluck pours himself a glass of orange juice. "Does it matter?"

"It matters to Grace," I say.

Cluck's blue eyes go cold for a moment and he sits down. Then he takes my fork, carefully scoops up some eggs, and holds them out for me to taste.

This is new; I open my mouth.

Cluck lifts the fork to my lips. The gesture is both demanding and delicate somehow; I didn't know Cluck did delicate.

He waits while I chew, then offers up another bite, which I take. The sunlight is warm through the window, and it's shimmering in Cluck's hair. The cold look has left his eyes. When the ice maker in the freezer gives a little roar I don't even jump. This is because I know the sounds of Cluck's kitchen like I know the sound of my own heartbeat.

He has collected more eggs onto the fork now, and suddenly I'm hungrier than I've ever been in my life. Cluck feeds me until there's not one speck of scrambled egg left on the plate.

"Thank you," I say.

Cluck nods. "Yow."

I get up and put the plate in the sink just as Mrs. McNally comes out of the bedroom in her bathrobe. Cluck is already getting more eggs out of the fridge.

Mrs. McNally gives me a hug. She is genuinely happy and surprised to see me, and it occurs to me that I haven't been around much lately.

"Maybe I'll come for dinner one night," I say, and I mean it. (Cluck's other specialty, believe it or not, is pesto sauce.)

He gets the eggs whisked, then walks me to the door. I step out onto the porch and turn back to face him.

"You were looking at me," I say softly, "when you were kissing Grace."

Cluck gives me a slow smile. "When I was kissing Grace," he says, pushing the hair out of his eyes, "you were looking at me."

I open my mouth, but I'm not sure how to respond to that. My best effort: "Whatever."

Cluck laughs. "Yeah. Whatever." Then he kisses

the tip of his finger and touches it to my nose. I smell cayenne pepper and garlic salt.

Sometimes, I really hate that guy.

* * *

Both Nat's parents are at work when I arrive at her house, but I know where they hide the key, so I let myself in and head for her room. Natalie, like any self-respecting, non-poetically-inclined teenager on the first Monday of summer vacation, is sound asleep.

"Are you awake?"

"Rrrrrggghhh."

I give her a little shove. This may sound cruel, but as her best friend, I'm well within my rights. "Get up."

Nat rolls over. "Why?"

I lie. "I feel like making French toast."

"So make it."

"We always make it together."

"Change is good, C.C."

"Fine." I stomp off and start opening cabinets in the kitchen. I've been best friends with Natalie for so long that I know where everything is. Ask me where her mother keeps the apple corer, and I can tell you. Ask me how far Nat's gone with Frankie Bruno, though, and I'm stumped. Where's the logic?

I'm flipping the first batch of toast when Nat drags herself into the kitchen. She looks at the clock. "Nine-fifteen. Mother of God."

It's times like this when I wish we drank coffee because right now would be a perfect moment to offer her a cup. But she's already chugging a can of diet root beer.

"I need you to take me shopping," I say, handing over a plate of French toast.

This intrigues her. "Yeah? For what?"

"Bras."

Nat gives me a look. "Bras?"

"Actually, one should be enough."

Natalie grins. Now she gets it. "A date bra."

"A date bra?" I'm not familiar with the term.

Nat spears a square of toast with her fork and nods. "That's what you want it for, isn't it? To impress Patrick."

I think my face is probably fuchsia. "Yes. Is that stupid?" This is uncharted territory for me.

"Not stupid at all. Come on." She gets up from the table, and I follow her back to her bedroom, where she pulls open a dresser drawer. "Date bras," she announces.

I pick one up. It's powder-blue satin, and the straps have scalloped edges. There's a pink one with lace cups, a white one with red ribbon accents, and a black one that shimmers in the light.

"Wow," is all I can think of to say.

"It's all about making an impression," Nat explains.

Suddenly, I have this vision of Natalie growing up and earning a fortune writing trashy romance novels, while I struggle in poverty, trying to get my poems published in obscure literary magazines. I'm convinced, by the way, that this is precisely the reason our relationship works.

I put back the bra. "You probably wouldn't recommend playing volleyball in any of these."

"No. But we aren't talking about volleyball, are we, C.C.?" Natalie grabs her bathrobe out of the closet. "We can go to Braddock's," she tells me and heads for the bathroom, leaving me to study the gentle science of lingerie. And for Nat it really is a science. The left-hand side of the drawer is all bras, folded and lined up according to some elaborate, fashion-based system known only to Nat. (For all I know, there's a rule that says you can't wear lace after Labor Day.) The right-hand side holds two neat rows of panties that correspond exactly with the bras—*matching* panties that, I assume, came with the date bras. The thought of date panties, I should tell you, scares me to death.

I slam the drawer closed and flop down onto the bed to wait for Nat to come out of the shower. My mind drifts in the direction of a poem, and I discover that there are very few words in the English language that rhyme with bra—there's "rah," which doesn't surprise me at all.

A hundred years later, Nat is standing in the doorway, dressed and ready.

She says, "Let's shop." It's Natalie's battle cry.

I get up from the bed and we're off. Date bra, here I come.

* * *

Braddock's is Natalie's favorite place on earth. We walk in and I expect the salespeople to call her by name. Personally, I like Braddock's, too. It reminds me of being little and going back-to-school shopping with my mom. There's this powdery, plastic smell and the sound of paper shopping bags being shaken open that really takes me back. Of course, since I've gone to Catholic school forever, my back-to-school shopping list never consisted of much more than knee socks and new shoes. But it was memorable, regardless.

Today, Nat and I shoot right by children's socks and shoes. She navigates the cosmetics counters and better sportswear, exuding confidence. She is in her element.

Suddenly, we're standing in a section that—were it not for the cash register and the headless, brassiere-clad mannequins—could be easily mistaken for a guest bedroom in the Palace of Versailles. There are lush draperies, lace-covered tables, and fancy armchairs holding piles of ruffled pillows. There are also garter belts that look like medieval torture devices.

"Lingerie," Nat announces.

"I never would have guessed."

"Shhhhh!"

"Nat, it's just the underwear department."

But Nat shushes me again; she takes her shopping seriously. "Do you want a date bra or not?" she asks me.

I nod. I'm relieved to see that there are not many shoppers in lingerie this morning. Nat steers me through pajamas and nightgowns to a long table that looks as if it might have been in Louis XIV's breakfast nook, prior to being purchased by Braddock's Department Store. What's on the table is an expanded version of Natalie's underwear drawer—bras and panties arranged in rows. When Nat explains that these items are sold separately,

I am overcome with relief. As I've said, date panties suggest an entire realm that I am not sure I'm prepared to consider.

I can only assume that Nat has those matching panties because she couldn't resist the allure of a coordinated set. I know I'm not ready to deal with any other explanation. *Anyway,* "sold separately" is like music to my ears. We're only here for a bra, thank goodness.

"What size?" she asks, and I tell her.

Nat finds the appropriate row and begins the search. She immediately eliminates anything white or beige, not to mention anything that looks as if it provides an iota of support. I should explain that my everyday, ordinary bras are really not bad; I mean they're not government-issue or anything. They're pretty and feminine, just not *overly.* I get the feeling that date bras should be as *overly* as possible.

Nat holds up a little satin number the color of pistachio ice cream.

"Green?" I ask.

"Sea foam," Nat corrects me.

I shake my head. She digs another few minutes, then presents an almost transparent lace bra for my approval.

"Beige?"

Nat rolls her eyes. "It's champagne."

Nat can be a snotty shopper. I study the bra. "It hooks in front."

"Is this a problem?"

She would know better than I. "Is it?"

Nat doesn't answer. She selects a pink bra with darker pink piping around the cups. I like it. It's not screaming "feel me up!" or "grope me!" It's what Nat would probably call "understated." "Is that a date bra?"

"It's close." She weeds out a semi-sheer black one with lace accents and satin straps. "*This* is the genuine article!"

"Wow." I never thought a piece of clothing could actually frighten me. "I don't think so, Nat."

"Just try it on." She hands me the three bras and pushes me toward the fitting room.

Nat waits outside the curtain while I go inside. I remove my shirt, then my own bra and try the beige—oops, sorry—*champagne* one first. It's pretty plungey and gives me a lot of cleavage, but the seams across the cups make my boobs look pointy. No thanks. The pink one is dull; it's the kind of bra you'd wear to a doctor's appointment. But the black one, the *scary* one, is not at all scary on. It's . . . well, it's sexy. There, I said it. It's sexy. It's black and it's sexy. Nat asks how it fits, and, since I refuse to say the word "sexy" out loud in a department store, I say, "Comfortable."

Nat knows me. She says, "We'll take it."

I get dressed and take the sexy black bra to the cash register. The lingerie section has become more crowded, and I'm eager to get out of there.

The cashier probably took this job for the employee discount on girdles. I'm about to hand her the bra when someone comes up beside me and says, "C.C.?"

I turn and look into the face of Sister Jude.

"I thought that was you." She gives me a smile. "How's everything?"

"Terrific."

Now picture the scene, if you will: I'm standing in the lingerie department purchasing what is, in all likelihood, the absolute sexiest bra in the history of underwear, and I'm having a conversation with a *nun.* I crumple the bra into a ball and hope she doesn't notice.

"I'm with my mother," Sister tells me. "She's shopping for a new bathrobe."

"That's nice." I wonder if she's telling me this in case I had mistakenly assumed she was buying underwear for herself. Not that I would have assumed that in a million years. I figure nuns' underwear is a strictly regulated commodity—it probably has to be approved by the Vatican.

The cashier is saying, "May I help you?"

If I hand over the bra, Sister will get a good, clear view of it. I'm sorry, but I'm not entirely comfortable with this. I showed her my poetry; that doesn't mean I want to show her my underwear.

I look at the woman and say, "You know what? I changed my mind. I'll return the item to the display table." Then I turn to my formerly favorite teacher and say, "Good-bye, Sister."

"So long, C.C."

I back away, keeping the bra out of sight. The cashier watches me to be sure I put it back on the table.

Nat is browsing in accessories. I tell her what happened. First she rolls her eyes. Then she cracks up.

"Now what?"

Nat has one word: "Catalogues!"

We leave Braddock's in a hurry, Natalie going over her mental inventory of mail-order lingerie, and me wishing just a little that we'd been shopping for knee socks.

* * *

Did I mention that Natalie got her first credit card the day she learned to walk? She's sitting on her bed holding a lingerie catalogue open in front of her. The phone is wedged between her ear and her shoulder, and she's reading the item number of my date bra to the operator. She tells the operator the shipping address is different from the billing address, and to ship it to C. Carruthers.

I whisper a reminder: "We need it by Friday."

"How long?" she asks the operator, then smiles at the answer. "Thank you." She hangs up the phone. "Wednesday. Guaranteed."

I take the catalogue and look at the bra we picked out. It's almost exactly like the one I didn't buy in front of Sister Jude. Nat says it's better quality, but I doubt very much that will matter to Patrick. I close the catalogue. "I need some advice," I tell Nat.

"Hand wash, line dry," she tells me.

"I wasn't talking about the bra."

"Oh." She looks as if she is about to say something extremely profound but the phone rings. It's Frankie. He's calling to ask if Nat wants to go to the movies tonight with Pat and me.

I say, "Pat and I are going to the movies tonight?" When you have an official boyfriend, life is full of surprises. According to Frankie, Pat's been calling me all morning.

Nat says, sure, she'll go, and then Frankie drops the bomb. Nat covers the mouthpiece to tell me what he just told her.

"Cluck and Kelly are coming, too."

My jaw drops.

Nat removes her hand from the mouthpiece to firm up the details with Frankie.

She hangs up and announces, "We're meeting at your house at six-thirty."

"*My* house?" Whose idea was this? "Why?"

"Because you live closest to the theater."

I can't argue; geography is against me. "Kelly Sinclair in my house," I say. I'm trying to picture it.

"It gets better," Nat tells me. "After the movie, we're going to Kelly's."

"Get out!"

Nat shrugs. "That's the plan."

"Get *out!*" This must be Cluck's doing. He's my best friend, but he can be a sadist sometimes. In this case, however, I can't decide whom he's trying to torture—me or Kelly.

"Will Tim be there?" I ask. I'm not hopeful, exactly, just curious.

Another shrug from Nat. Then she checks the

clock. It's twelve-thirty, which means we've only got six hours to get ready. For Nat, this is cutting it close.

I walk home slowly. It's a perfect, summery, blue-lit day. I remember being little and walking to Natalie's and thinking she lived halfway across the universe. Three blocks, when you're five, feels like miles. On weekends, my father would walk me. He'd hold my hand, and it never occurred to me to be embarrassed about it. The fact that I'm walking now, on the very same sidewalk, sends a strange shiver through me.

I was six the first time I decided to walk to Natalie's alone. My parents and I had just come home from our vacation at some boardwalk resort, and I was in a big hurry to show Nat my new sandals. (I guess even then she was the authority.) Dad said he would stand at the end of the driveway and watch me as far as the first hydrant, which was at the corner by Cluck's house, if Natalie's mom would stand on her front sidewalk and wait for me.

I remember I was so excited to be walking alone in those sandals, that I took off, leaving my father at the end of the driveway. When I rounded the corner, though—terror. In my heart, I knew Dad was still standing there. But I couldn't see him, and he couldn't see me, and there were at least two more hydrants to go before I'd be able to spot Natalie's mom. I remember I wanted to turn around and run home faster than I'd ever run in my life, and I didn't care what kind of damage it might do to those stupid sandals. I was afraid.

But now I'm reaching for another part of the same memory—something hazy in the peripheral vision of my mind's eye. I try to make it out, but it disappears.

What I do remember is that I *didn't* turn around and run, because, for some reason, the terror disappeared as quickly as it had come. Something made the terror go away. My guess is, the hazy part of the memory is that something. And I think I must have recognized it then, but I don't—I can't—now.

So I keep walking. I'm just about to my house when I notice Curtis Piperfield, changing a bicycle tire in his driveway. I haven't talked to him in a while so I decide to kill some time and cross the street.

"Hey, Curtis."

He glances up from the spokes. "Hi, C.C."

"Where's Bridget?"

He shrugs. "Where's Patrick?"

I shrug. It bothers me a little that these the are first things we think of to say to one another.

There's more to me than Patrick, isn't there? I guess when you're part of a high-profile couple, people forget how to think of you as a solo performer. This realization bothers me more than a little, and I think about how I used to like listening to Curtis play guitar, before he gave it up for Bridget.

"I was wondering something. Do you miss playing your guitar?"

He hesitates. "Yeah. I miss it."

I say, "I miss it, too."

Curtis stops spinning the wheel and looks at me. He doesn't say anything, but he looks sort of grateful. I'm trying to imagine how I would feel if Patrick wanted me to give up poetry. Not that I would, of course. That's why I've always been kind of disappointed in Curtis for caving in on this issue. But I still miss his music.

"See ya, Curtis."

"Bye, C.C."

I cross the street again and check the mailbox. The day I left for Natalie's, the day I crossed half the universe, I couldn't even reach it, and suddenly I'm wondering whatever happened to those stupid sandals anyway.

It's funny how the most perfect days can also turn out to be the most confusing.

Chapter 7

Patrick arrives at my house at six-thirty sharp. The first thing I say is, "Whose idea was this?"

"Mostly Cluck's," Pat confesses. "Maybe he wants you and Kelly to be friends."

"He should start with something easy," I tell him. "Like world peace."

Patrick follows me into the family room and shakes hands with my father. My mother comes out of the kitchen with a plate of cookies, and I immediately send her back. Is she trying to destroy me socially, or what?

Then Nat and Frankie arrive. I can't help wondering whether Nat is wearing a date bra. Not that it would matter. I think kids stopped fooling around in movie theaters back in the seventies. Then again, I'm not exactly a specialist in this area.

The doorbell rings and Pat offers to answer it, which I can tell my mother finds utterly sweet. He returns with Cluck and Kelly in tow.

"Hi."

"Hi."

"Hi."

"Hi."

"Hi."

Cluck doesn't bother saying hi to me. He does say "Yow" to my parents, though. Prep school manners. Plus, Cluck loves my mom and dad and they're crazy about him. I can tell my mom is surprised to see Cluck with someone other than Grace, but she doesn't say anything. If she offers anyone a cookie, I'll run away from home.

The boys talk baseball with my father for a few minutes, and if that's not the ultimate irony, I don't know what is. Then, since it's my house, I say, "Well . . ." which gets everyone heading toward the door.

But just when I think I'm out of the woods, my father says, "Take a jacket, C.C."

I tell him, "It's warm out."

"It'll be cool later on."

"But Dad . . ."

"Take a jacket, C.C."

I'm furious now. Kelly isn't wearing a jacket, not even a peach-colored one. Natalie has a sweater tied around her waist, but that's not the same as wearing a jacket. Still, in the interest of avoiding a war and getting out the door, I grab a jacket from the hall closet. I'm so flustered I'm not even sure if it's one of mine.

"Happy now?" There is no way to say this without sounding disrespectful.

Dad gives me a cold look. But all he says is, "Eleven-thirty."

When we get outside, I look at the jacket I'm holding. It's a beat-up old denim jacket that's been hanging in our closet since Cluck left it at my house a year ago. Natalie gives it an approving look; I happen to know that she believes denim, like navy blue, goes with everything.

We start out for the movies and the tension lifts. Patrick and I are holding hands. Frankie and Nat are holding hands. Kelly is *trying* to get Cluck to hold her hand. By the time we reach Durgan's Pharmacy, he's given in, and they're holding hands, too.

I give a fleeting thought to Grace and feel a little guilty, but if she makes the cheerleading squad, she'll be hanging out with Kelly more than I do.

All's fair in love and organized sports, I guess.

* * *

The movie is horrible. Cluck throws candy all over the place in protest. Natalie can't get past the fact that they don't sell diet root beer at the candy counter. And you know what? I'm glad I have the denim jacket, because it's maybe twelve below zero in the theater. I'd never admit this to my father, though. And don't even start with me, because, be honest, neither would you!

* * *

One hundred and fifteen minutes later the movie is finally over and we leave the theater. Kelly Sinclair has a popcorn kernel stuck to her front tooth. I can tell Nat notices, too, but neither one of us is about to tell Kelly. There—Grace has been avenged.

Outside, the sky is a glossy black lacquer, and it's significantly warmer than it was inside. Immediately, I shrug off the jacket, and immediately Cluck snatches it away.

"Mine," he says. The word seems to echo, and I wonder if it's just the jacket he's talking about.

"How are we getting to Kelly's?" Frankie asks.

It's a good question; Kelly's house is well beyond walking distance. Everyone turns to her.

She opens with a giggle and checks her watch. "My brother's going to pick us up."

I think I'm the only one who hears Patrick mumble, "Terrific," under his breath. I *know* I'm the only one who gets a discreet kick to the ankle from Nat. Talk about your awkward situations!

We loiter in front of the movie theater a good ten minutes before Tim pulls up in a compact car. Cluck hops into the front seat, and Kelly climbs, giggling, onto his lap. Nat and Frankie and Pat and I crowd into the back.

It's impossible to miss the fact that Tim Sinclair is shirtless. His hair is wet, and he looks like an ad for some designer men's cologne. He smells like one, too—a fresh, woodsy fragrance. If *handsome* had a scent, this would be it.

Tim explains that he was at open rec at Simon Pete's gym and only had five minutes to shower before he came to get us. "Hardly had time to dry off," he tells us, which seems to me a very personal topic of conversation.

When we pile out at Kelly's, Tim gives me a smile. I smile back, in what I hope is a very general way. "How was the movie?" he asks me.

I say, "Pathetic," and get into the house fast.

Tim gets his basketball from the trunk and dribbles in behind us.

I've only been in Kelly Sinclair's house once before, and that was for her eighth birthday party. It was a Barbie theme, if I remember correctly, and her mother did everyone's nails and put our hair in upsweeps. Clearly, those were Kelly's formative years; they certainly left their mark.

Kelly takes us downstairs to the finished basement: The Sinclair Family Hall of Fame. There are shelves full of Tim's trophies, and the walls are covered with framed photos of him playing basketball for Prep and of Kelly in every cheerleading uniform it has ever been her pleasure to wear.

At one end of the room there's a pool table, which means the boys are out of the picture.

Pat says, "Rack 'em," and Cluck starts juggling billiard balls.

There's a love seat and two chairs. Nat and I grab the chairs. Kelly turns on the stereo, then comes back and sits down on the love seat.

There is not a single thing in the world I can think of to say to her.

Nat, on the other hand, comes right out with it. "How's Grace doing at cheerleading?"

Kelly blinks but keeps grinning. ("Pretend it

doesn't bother you" is the pep squad credo, remember?) "She's got a really good chance of making it," she tells us. "Really good."

I can tell, by the way she obviously hates saying this, that it's actually true. Good for Grace—if this is what she wants. Besides, I know it'll just kill Kelly, so I'm even almost happy about it. Almost.

Then Cluck is saying, "I'm damn thirsty. How about a Coke?"

I have to bite my lip to keep from scolding him. That's Kelly's job now, although if I ever heard her do it, I think I'd slap her face.

She gets up, but since she knows the minute she leaves the basement, Nat and I will talk about her, she gives us this big smile and says, "Come on."

We have no choice but to follow her. The minute we hit the kitchen, I see Tim. He is scooping cherry vanilla ice cream into a bowl. He's still topless, and his biceps jump with every scoop. He looks up from the bowl and gives me this very spectacular grin.

"I hear that you write poetry," he says.

"You *heard* that?"

"I told him," says Kelly.

"Oh."

I'm not stupid; I know that Kelly telling her brother I write poetry is in no way an attempt to flatter me. Quite the contrary; there's no question that Kelly thought she was revealing my dirtiest secret. (Imagine her saying, "C.C. writes poetry" in the same tone of voice she'd use to say, "C.C. doesn't shave her armpits," and then you'll understand her purpose.)

She shakes some ice into a glass.

"Who told you?" I ask her.

"Cluck."

Tim puts the ice cream away and takes a seat at the table. "My host family in England was big on early nineteenth-century poetry," he says. "Keats, Shelley . . ."

"Byron," I add, effectively slicing Kelly out of the conversation.

Tim smiles.

"Do they play basketball in Europe?" asks Nat.

"They do," says Tim, swirling some cherry vanilla around on his spoon. "I didn't."

I'm interested. "Why not?"

"Because I didn't have to," Tim says, shrugging. Suddenly, in spite of the fact that he's sitting in his own kitchen, he looks a little homesick.

"Going back?" I ask.

"I never left." It's a cryptic answer, but a flicker of understanding passes between us. He smiles.

"It's all about independence," he says. "But then, I guess you know how that feels."

For some reason, I am really, really flattered. "Yeah," I tell him. "I guess I do."

Nat and Kelly collect the Cokes and glasses and head down to the basement, but I hang back. Tim looks as if there's more he'd like to say to me, and I know I look as if I'd like to hear it.

"You going out for cheerleading?" he asks.

"No," I answer quickly.

Tim looks relieved. "I didn't actually think you were," he says, as if he's afraid he might have insulted me.

"I'm just here by some cruel twist of popularity," I tell him.

He's looking at me kind of closely.

"You okay?" he asks, cocking an eyebrow.

This throws me. "Sure. Fine." I return the eyebrow thing. "Don't I look fine?" I regret that as soon as I say it, since it sounds like one of Grace's fishing-for-compliments lines.

"You look incredible," Tim says, grinning. "Just a little lonely."

(He's good.) "Side effect of independence," I answer truthfully.

And the next thing I know, I'm sitting across

from Tim at the same table where, in some other lifetime, I ate birthday cake off a Barbie plate, and I'm telling him everything—about Grace going out for cheerleading and Sister Jude selling out, about the fragile condition of my friendship with Cluck, about Pat and his highly organized approach to romance. Something just draws the words out of me—something other than Tim's sexy good looks and warm, warm eyes. And the way he listens goes way beyond the realm of prep school manners, beyond just being polite. He actually seems to care. Or understand. Or both. Somehow, he knows what questions to ask, and here, of all places, I seem strangely closer to the answers.

Eventually, the conversation winds down and we share a pleasant silence. Then I say, "Pat's probably wondering . . ."

And Tim says, "He probably is."

A moment later, I return to the basement, where the guys have quit playing pool and are now having a one-arm push-up competition in the middle of the floor. This is the price we pay for going out with jocks. Kelly finds it giggle-worthy. Nat rolls her eyes.

Pat gives me a curious look; I respond with an innocent smile. He frowns and continues his push-ups.

I sink into the chair beside Nat, letting the ordinary stuff go on around me. Talking to Tim was a very satisfying experience—different (not better, not worse) than talking to Cluck or Nat. The only way I can describe it is that I feel as if my brain has been making out.

Not bad for a Monday night.

* * *

At eleven-fifteen, we're waiting for Frankie's mom on the Sinclairs' front porch. (I've escaped with Cluck's jean jacket; he saw me take it but didn't protest.)

Mrs. Bruno lets me and Pat off at my house at eleven-thirty exactly. My parents are not waiting up, which is a sign of trust. We go inside to the family room. Pat's curfew is midnight; there is still a serious double standard operating among Catholics, and boys getting an extra half hour is only the tip of the iceberg. (Don't get me started.)

We sit on the couch. There's only one lamp on, so we have perfect kissing ambiance. But Pat is a little chilly, and I know it's because of Tim.

So I kiss first. I'm amazed at how quickly Pat loosens up. I must be an even better kisser than I thought. Either that, or jealousy really fires up a guy.

101

We kiss for a long time, and I mean we really *kiss.* Pat sort of leans into me until I'm lying down, and then he maneuvers himself so that he is lying beside me. If you've never been kissed lying down, I highly recommend it. We've only tried this once before, so we're a little clumsy at first. We get our legs tangled, but that turns out to be a good thing, and once he gets his elbow out of my rib cage, we're set.

I wonder if this is my best bet for Friday; will the lying-down position adequately showcase my date bra? I'll have to check with Natalie, although she's likely to say something magazine-ish, like "It may interrupt the fluid lines of the fabric and detract from the simple elegance of the lingerie."

I'm thinking this and kissing like crazy, so it takes me a second to realize that all of a sudden there's more than one lamp on.

Pat and I sit up fast. Unfortunately, not fast enough.

My father is standing in the doorway with his hand on the light switch. And he doesn't say a word.

In fact, no one says a word.

My father looks at me—not Patrick, just me—then he walks away.

Patrick is in a panic. "What should we do?"

I say, "What can we do?" I'm calm, in a very weird way. So I'm surprised to discover that I'm crying. Not hysterically, just softly. The tears seem to be handling this one on their own.

"Should we apologize?"

"For kissing? That would sound kind of dumb, don't you think?" I certainly think so.

"So what should we do?"

I shrug, rub some tears off my cheeks, and point out to Patrick that it's ten past twelve. He gets up. I walk him to the door and go up on my toes to kiss him. He looks a little surprised at this, but I figure we're pretty much past the point of no return, so why not?

"Call me," he says. "As soon as . . ." But he's not sure how to finish.

"Good night."

"Night."

He takes a backward step out onto the porch; his eyes are wishing me luck.

But I don't need luck. I need a miracle.

Chapter 8 ———————

My phone rings the next morning at seven a.m. "Hello?"

"Good morning, C.C.," comes a pleasant voice through the receiver. I recognize it right away.

"Hi, Mrs. Boccaluzzo."

"Is Grace up?"

Does she want me to guess? "Um . . ."

"I thought I should give her an early wake-up call," she says brightly.

Now I'm catching on. Grace must have told her mother she was sleeping over. "Right," I say through a big swallow. "Early."

I can hear Mrs. Boccaluzzo sipping her coffee on the other end of the line. "Didn't she tell you? She has a dentist appointment at nine-fifteen."

"Oh." That's not all she didn't tell me. (Double negative; *damn* you Grace!)

"I'm going to have to come by for her early, though, because the brakes on my car are squeaking again, and the service department at the dealership promised me a loaner car if I can get mine in before nine."

"Sounds like a very reliable dealership," I say, stalling.

"Yes." Mrs. Boccaluzzo pauses for another hit of coffee. "May I speak to Grace?"

"She's . . ." *Think fast, C.C.* "She's in the shower."

I promise Mrs. Boccaluzzo that I'll relay the message and that Grace will be on my front steps at eight-forty. Then I slam the phone down, pick it up again, and dial Cluck.

"Yow?"

"Where's Grace?"

"Don't you mean 'where's *Kelly*'?"

Smartass. "No, Cluck, I mean, where's *Grace!* She told her mother she was sleeping here."

"How the hell do I know where Grace is?" he grumbles, but something in the grumble tells me he has a hunch.

I wait.

"Get dressed," he tells me. "Call Nat."

I hang up the phone. Then I call Nat.

"Hmmmm?"

"Hi. It's me."

I hear Nat roll over, I suppose to check her clock. "Mother of God, C.C. It's only five after seven."

"I'm well aware of the time, thank you," I snap, then cut right to the chase. "Grace told her mom she was sleeping at my house last night."

"Hmm." I can hear Nat throwing aside her sheets. "Pretty clever, for Grace."

I cut her off before she can tell me how well Grace would do in public school. "She didn't mention any of it to me," I say.

"Not so clever."

"Get dressed. I'll pick you up in ten minutes."

Nat says sure, then hangs up. In a show of trust, or perhaps ESP, she doesn't ask me why she should get dressed. This is either because she knows what I'm planning to do—i.e., go find Grace—or simply because, as my best friend, she is sworn to do my bidding without question. Maybe both.

To save time, I hurry into the same clothes I wore the night before. I have this inane thought that Nat will most definitely *not* put on the same clothes she wore the night before. For all I know, there is a whole portion of her wardrobe she saves for situations like this. Crisis attire, or something.

I shoot off a quick note to my parents, something about a morning jog with Nat, and head for the front door. It's cool out so I grab the jean jacket. Cluck is just rounding the corner toward my driveway. He looks serious and concerned, and I can't tell if it's because he doesn't know where Grace is, or because he does.

Without a word, we walk to Nat's, and she's waiting on the sidewalk. Cluck turns on his heel and heads back in the direction we came. I don't even notice what Nat's wearing; I happen to be scared to death.

* * *

"You know where she is," I say to Cluck. It's a statement, not a question.

He nods and keeps walking.

"So tell us," says Nat. "Is she okay?"

Cluck throws off an icy shrug. "That's up to her." Then he closes his mouth and doesn't say another word.

We follow him in silence past St. Bernadette's for Girls and keep walking until we reach the driveway of St. Simon Peter's Boys' Prep. It's a tall, imposing building; the spiny spires seem to reach upward for miles, piercing the sky. Cluck stops abruptly at the entrance, and I crash right into him.

"She's here?"

"Most likely."

"Why is she here?"

"Summer school." Cluck gives me a look with a piece of a smile in it.

"Funny." Under the circumstances, I feel a stab of guilt for liking the smile. "Why is she really here?"

"Football camp."

"Cluck!"

"No," says Nat, pointing across Simon Pete's quad toward the old dormitory. "I think he's serious."

I turn and look. When my father went to Prep three billion years ago, it was a boarding school, which is why there is a dorm on campus. Presently, the school uses it to host visiting priests and brothers and . . .

"Football camp? Grace is *here?*"

"Don't say she's working on her spiral pass," warns Nat.

Cluck has two words for us. "Billy Dennon." Then he does the most incredible thing: He leaves.

Nat and I stare after him a moment. Cluck and Grace have broken up, you'll recall, so the fact that he's involved himself this far is exceedingly chivalrous. But he's leaving Nat and me alone . . . at football camp. Is he crazy?

"Cluck!"

He doesn't stop.

I turn to Nat. "Looks like we're going to football camp," I tell her. But I think she already knows that.

"If anyone asks, we're somebody's sister."

Nat gives me a look. "Who's gonna ask?"

She's probably right. A bunch of football players, in all their mesh-shirted majesty, are already lined up and stretching out on the quad, and I can tell from the way they're looking at us that none of them would really care. They see two beyond-reasonably-attractive girls cutting through their morning calisthenics; why we are there, or to whom we might be genetically bound, is not likely to concern them.

"We're outnumbered," Nat whispers.

Tell me something I don't know. I could strangle Cluck for feeding us to the lions like this.

The warm-up is being led by a guy who's maybe five minutes older than the players—not a coach, a coachling. A college guy, maybe. A real coach, an adult, would certainly inquire as to what business Nat and I had at football camp at the crack of dawn and would more than likely toss us out. The coachling, however, does nothing to stop us. Instead, he winks at us and gives us this cocky little grin—without even missing a jumping jack.

"Do you see Billy?" I whisper to Nat.

She reviews the troops, then shakes her head. We head for the dorm.

I have only a vague recollection of what Billy Dennon looks like, but Nat could probably do a police sketch of him. She had the extreme good fortune to be a seventh-grader at Miltondale Junior High the year Billy was a ninth-grader there. After that, his parents shipped him off to high school at Immaculate Heart, two towns over, which is the best football school in the area. We've all heard of Billy, though: A) because he's cute, and B) because he's a football icon. He'll be a senior next year, and he's been a fixture at Prep's annual summer football camp forever. I have no idea where, when, or how Grace Boccaluzzo happened to meet him.

I don't have time to dwell on that.

In case you'd forgotten, Nat and I are alone in a veritable sea of adrenaline-pumped high-school males with no adult supervision save Winky the Coachling, who has proven himself an unworthy chaperon. The fact that it's broad daylight does little to calm me down; this is a patently stupid position to be in. I really feel like murdering Cluck for deserting us.

The side door to the dorm is open, and I see a couple of boys in cut-off sweat pants and official camp T-shirts leaning there. They look to be about sixteen. One is tossing a football up and down. The other one whistles at us.

In a show of courage (or idiocy), Nat says, "Nice shirt," to the whistler.

"Do you know Billy Dennon?" I ask. My voice sounds a little rusty. I'm nervous.

The guy who didn't whistle gives me this lop-sided grin. "Fourth door on the right."

Natalie is really eyeing their shirts. I grab her arm and we head down the hall. The place smells like cologne and old sweat socks, and from behind a couple of doors I hear music blaring. We stop at the fourth one. There's a jockstrap hanging on the doorknob. It's not just revolting, it's confusing.

"What do you think?" I ask Nat, keeping my voice low.

She shrugs. "Must be some kind of signal."

Football camp's version of a DO NOT DISTURB sign? She's probably right.

I knock.

Nothing.

I knock again, clear my throat. "Grace?"

There is a half-gasp, half-shriek sound from inside the room. "C.C.?"

"Let's go," I tell her.

Through the door, I can hear the muffled sounds of conversation. Billy Dennon, for what it's worth, has a very deep and sexy voice. He's asking Grace to stay.

"Forget it," I say, loudly. "Let's go, Grace."

Nat rolls her eyes. We wait a few minutes, presumably for Grace to get dressed. I feel Promiscuous by Association. The guys in the doorway are watching us, but in a curious, polite sort of way. Still, I'm embarrassed.

Grace emerges at last, looking worse for wear, believe me. Billy Dennon, that jerk, doesn't even bother to walk her to the door. I shoot her a look of fury, to which she responds with a giggle! I stomp down the hall and she follows. So does Nat.

"How'd you find me?" Grace asks—too casually for my taste.

I stop and stare at her. "Your mother called me; I called Cluck."

Her face goes white. I'm not sure if it's the mention of her mom or of Cluck that does it. Then I fill her in on the situation with her mother's brakes, and she really starts to panic.

"Eight-forty?" she says. "But it's already seven-fifty. And I need time to shower."

I couldn't agree with her more. "Maybe Billy can give us a ride," I say coldly.

Grace shakes her head. "I don't want to get him mad."

Nat rolls her eyes. "God forbid."

Grace says she'll call Lisa Bruno, who's had her

license for almost a month. I'm not at all certain Lisa Bruno is going to come to the rescue, and the fact that Grace seems totally confident that she will really bugs me. Personally, I think Grace is delusional. Lisa Bruno doesn't have an unselfish bone in her body. But it occurs to me that maybe Grace needs a ride from *Lisa* almost as desperately as she needs a ride—meaning, she wants Lisa to see her here, to witness this, to smell Billy Dennon's cologne while it's still fresh on her skin. (Yuck.)

But since we have no other choice, we ask the guys in the cut-off sweats if there's a pay phone nearby. The whistler says the closest one is in the gym, and he and his buddy offer to walk us there. You've got to admit, there's something chivalrous about it, and it only serves to increase this urge I'm having to run back inside, kick down Billy Dennon's door, and strangle him in his bed.

We head for the gym and as we get closer, I hear the sound of basketballs thumping.

"Morning rec," one of the guys explains.

"Rec?" I say it like a prayer of thanks, and suddenly there is this incredible, ethereal lightness inside me—because somehow I know . . . I just *know.* I hurry ahead of the others and open the door of the gym.

Tim Sinclair looks up from the foul line. He's a little shocked to see me, naturally, but I can tell he's trying not to show it. He releases the ball into the air; it swishes through the net, and he gives me a smile.

I'm overwhelmed by it—not because it's gorgeous (which it is), but because of the relief that washed over me. "We need a ride," I say in a shaky voice. Then, since I've got some Catholic-school manners of my own, I add, "Please."

"Sure," Tim says. He doesn't ask any questions. He just grabs the basketball, tucks it under his arm, and follows me out of the gym. There is something utterly respectful about that, if you ask me.

Tim is big, even compared to the football players, and the whistler and his buddy both take a step back when they see him. I thank them for their efforts, and Tim, Grace, and I head for the parking lot. Nat hangs back for a moment.

"You okay?" Tim asks me when we reach the car.

I nod. Grace is climbing into the back seat. I get in the front. When Nat catches up, she slides in next to Grace, and I'm not surprised to see that she is now the proud owner of a St. Simon Peter's Football Camp T-shirt.

Tim starts driving; I tell him where I live, and when we're safely off the Simon Pete's campus, I turn in my seat to give Grace a good glare.

"Tell me," I say.

"Tell you what?"

"How did Cluck know?"

She gives me a blank look.

Getting a straight answer from Grace is becoming more difficult by the day. Then it dawns on me. "That's why Cluck broke up with you," I breathe. "Because he caught you sneaking around with Billy."

Grace's eyes dart sideways, but there's no skirting this one. She gives me a reluctant nod.

"You said he said *he* wanted to see other people!"

"He did," she mutters defensively. "He said that *after* he found out I was already seeing Billy."

I could slug her! "You left that part out."

Grace shrugs, and suddenly there's nothing on earth I want more than to see Grace make cheerleading. The rest of the ride is silent.

When Tim pulls up to my house, Grace is out of the car practically before it stops; Nat follows at a less insane pace. I just sort of sit there in the front seat; I'm so lost in my outrage that it takes me a while to notice that Tim is staring at me.

"Thank you," I say. It's all-inclusive.

"No problem. Is she okay?"

"Mostly," I say with a nice dollop of sarcasm, but, of course, he doesn't get the reference. We sit quietly a moment, the way we did last night at his kitchen table, and that reminds me of something.

"You said it felt good not to have to play basketball," I say softly.

He nods. "I did things in Europe that had nothing to do with basketball, and nobody was surprised or disappointed."

I'm trying to imagine Tim Sinclair—who, until recently, I'd only associated with a number and a varsity jacket—sitting in some Italian piazza or walking along the Seine. I have to work to keep a basketball out of the picture, and that's when I see what he's getting at.

"Then why were you playing this morning?" I ask. "And last night, at rec?"

He gives me this cute, boyish lift of his shoulders, the closest he's come to looking shy around me. "I still love the game—when it's just me and the ball and the net and the rhythm."

Except for the part about the ball and the net, that could be me talking about writing poetry. Me and the words and the page and the rhythm. "I know what you mean," I tell him. "Independence . . ."

"Independence."

"Like in Europe."

"Like in here." Tim gently taps his finger over my heart, and it's not in the least like second base. "That's what attracted me to you, C.C."

I would have guessed my hair. "Really?"

He gives me a sweetened-up boy version of Nat's eye roll. "Sounds corny, huh?"

"That's what made you sit with me at the burger place?" I ask. "My sense of freedom?"

"Well, yeah." He gives me half a smile. "That . . . and your hair." Tim adjusts the collar of my jean jacket; there's something protective in the gesture. "When I saw you at Mass—okay, sure—the first thing I thought was, hey, she's gorgeous. But once we started talking, I knew you and I were kindred spirits." He hesitates, only a second, and I know he's pleased at not having to define the term for me. "The world is full of kids in uniforms, C.C. It gets a little one-dimensional. A little . . ."—he searches for the right word—

" . . . Arranged." I sigh. Like getting to second base before sophomore year, I think. Like not talking to other boys on the phone. Like saying I love you because it's time.

Tim nods.

Suddenly, I have this crazy impulse to hug him, so I do. He returns the hug. It's got this brotherly current running through it.

Tim tells me he's going back to Europe for the summer.

"When do you leave?"

"The fourth."

"Of July?"

He nods, and we both smile at the significance of that, although it's nice that neither of us needs to point it out. He grabs a piece of paper and a pen from the glove compartment and writes down his European address.

"Be in touch," he says, as I tuck the address into my jacket pocket.

I give him my most independent smile. "You, too."

I wait for him to pull away before I turn to go inside. Not that I want to; not that I wouldn't mind going over to Cluck's for some scrambled eggs, or even just standing at the curb, looking at Curtis Piperfield's house for the rest of the day. I guess that's because right now I need everything to be the way it used to be, even if it's only for a moment or so. I need things to feel familiar. This whole Grace business has floored me, if you want to know the truth. Right now I know Grace Boccaluzzo less well than anyone else on earth.

I turn and head up the driveway to my house. It's been a very long morning.

Chapter 9

When Grace and Nat are gone, I lie down on my bed and immediately fall asleep. My mom looks in on me at noon to see if I'm alive.

From under the covers I assure her that I am, and she leaves. I sit up, rubbing my eyes. It takes me a while to sort through the events of the morning. Cluck . . . Grace . . . Billy Dennon (jerk!) . . . the football campers . . . Tim Sinclair. Then the fact that Pat and I got caught making out last night comes screeching to the forefront of my memory.

I go to Nat's and fill her in over some French toast. I start with my discussion with Tim at the Sinclairs' kitchen table, because for one thing, I like to tell stories in order of increasing importance, and for another, I simply don't have the energy for jumping right in with the part about getting caught kissing.

"So Tim *hates* basketball?"

"No," I tell her. "He didn't say that. He just said it's nice not to have to play."

Nat is pulling her newly acquired football camp T-shirt out of the dryer. "And Tim, unlike every other boy on earth, was not attracted to you because of your perfect face, your killer figure, or your gorgeous hair?"

I can't help blushing. "He did sort of like the hair."

"But he liked your . . . what was it? . . . your *independence* better?"

I shrug.

"Hmmmf." Nat gives me a friendly smirk. "So this guy wouldn't know a date bra if it hit him in the face."

I don't answer. My guess is, Tim Sinclair would definitely know a date bra when he saw one—he'll just never be seeing one on me. And do you know something? I prefer it that way. Moving on . . .

"What's Grace's story?" asks Nat. "Why would she go after Billy Dennon, when she already had Cluck?"

"Don't know."

I think back to when Grace and Cluck first got together. It was only a few months ago at the Spring Formal, but right now it feels like a lifetime. That was the first time I'd ever seen Grace exude any kind of confidence; it was like something contagious that she had come down with the minute Cluck asked her to dance.

I remind Nat and she laughs.

"Didn't last long," I sigh.

"Grace dating Cluck?"

"Grace having confidence."

"You'd think dating Cluck would have made her terminally confident," Nat observes. "She certainly *looked* confident whenever they were making out at the burger place."

"She looked *something*," I concede. "I'm not sure it was confident, though."

"What do you mean?"

"She knew she was with Cluck, and she knew that *we* knew she was with Cluck. I just don't think she ever really *believed* it."

Nat gives me a look. "Cluck doesn't strike me as the type whose kisses could be considered imaginary."

I refrain from comment; I have my own theories about Cluck's kisses.

"Grace had Cluck," Nat argues. "In her eyes, that meant she had everything."

I shrug. "Having everything is different from *keeping* everything."

"Which means. . . ?" Nat lifts an eyebrow at me.

I could explain it with a metaphor about the difference between writing my first poem and writing my second poem: Once I knew the first one was good, writing the next one took on a kind of urgency; could I pull it off again, or was that first one just a fluke?

Instead, I decide to go with a metaphor she'll truly respect: "Cluck," I tell her, "was Grace's first little black dress."

"The little black dress . . ." Nat's eyes flicker with recognition. "Elegant, flattering, comfortable, and not likely ever to go out of style."

"Right. But Billy . . . Billy was more like an impulse purchase, like a really trendy accessory she had to have, just to prove she had cutting-edge style, even though she knew it might spoil the perfect simplicity of the little black dress."

"I get it," Nat says. "But what I don't see is why Cluck didn't just tell us that Grace was two-timing him, instead of letting everyone think he dumped her and then came to the party with Kelly."

"I'm still working on that one."

She tugs the T-shirt over her head. "Frankie's gonna croak!" she says triumphantly.

I frown and suddenly find myself wishing she'd give old Frankie a break. I don't mention it, though, just follow her to her room. "Do you think I should yell at Cluck?"

"Sure," says Nat. "Yell at Cluck." She's looking over her shoulder in the mirror to see how the T-shirt looks from behind. "What are you going to yell about?"

"Leaving us!"

"Oh." She tugs at the neckline a little, then rolls up the sleeves. "We survived, though."

"I know that. I'm just questioning his loyalty."

"Ha!" Nat faces me. "Cluck's loyal to the bone. This morning had nothing to do with loyalty."

She's right. Loyalty's the wrong word. "Responsibility, then. I'm questioning his sense of responsibility."

"Question Grace's."

Bull's eye!

Nat is changing the T-shirt. I'm pleased to see she's putting on Frankie's baseball shirt; it says BRUNO across the back.

I flop down on her bed. "Do you think she and Billy were . . . you know."

"It wouldn't surprise me."

"I wonder if she loves him."

"Who could love a guy with a jockstrap on his doorknob?"

"Grace, maybe."

"Maybe." She crosses the room and looks at me with great seriousness. "Let's make a pact." (This will be our five millionth pact. It's a friend thing.) "If Patrick ever hangs a jockstrap on his doorknob, the relationship is over."

"I swear it," I say, smiling.

"And if Frankie ever hangs a jockstrap on his doorknob, he's history, too." She turns away extra fast, and I think it's because this is the closest she's ever come to proclaiming Frankie's significance. For some reason, it does my heart good.

Finally, I get to the part about Patrick and me getting caught kissing on the couch, and Nat gives me a "Mother of God." I'm happy to hear it—as I said before, I'm in need of things familiar today.

Then Nat tells me some kissing stories of her own, and we speculate about what Grace (after her night with Billy) would be able to add to the conversation. It's a very relaxing way to kill an afternoon, and considering that I'm going to have to face my dad sooner or later, I need all the relaxation I can get.

Chapter 10

I get home about ten minutes before my father does. This is careful scheduling on my part; I figure ten minutes alone with Mom to talk about last night is exactly enough.

I find her out back, watering the rhododendron. "Hi."

"Hi." She looks at me, then her concentration shifts to the willow tree. A small breeze moves the long yellow branches. They seem to drip from the sky. Finally, Mom looks back at me and smiles, which I figure is a good sign.

"Daddy planted that tree on your first birthday," she says. She tells me this as if she hasn't told me thirty-eight billion times before, as if she thinks I've forgotten.

"Are you on my side?" I ask her. "Or his?"

"I'm not on anyone's *side,* C.C." She comes over to me and puts her hands on my shoulders. "It's not about taking sides."

I feel this edge of anger creeping up. "Why was he spying on us?"

"He wasn't." Mom laughs, and I must say, I find it very inappropriate. "Believe me, C.C., he didn't want to catch you even more than you didn't want to be caught."

Double negatives again. It takes me a minute to do the verbal math. "Does he hate me?"

"No."

"Is he mad?"

Mom thinks for a minute. "It's complicated."

I'm thinking, *You're telling me!* but I say, "It used to be better."

"It used to be easier."

She's got a point. "So he's not mad?"

"Not in the traditional sense. But he's going to seem mad."

I'm not stupid. I know that seeming mad is just as bad as being mad. Anyway you look at it, I'm in trouble.

I hear Dad's car. A moment later he's banging out the back door, looking as if he wants to get this over with in a hurry. Fine with me. I give him a little wave: *Those of us about to be grounded salute you.*

He loosens his tie and looks a little bit lost, as if he doesn't recognize the back yard. Or maybe it's one of the people in the back yard that he just can't seem to place. He looks beyond me to the willow tree. "I'm not going to punish you," he says.

This knocks me out. "You're not?"

Dad shakes his head. "I'm just going to ask you a favor."

That could mean anything from more yard work to joining a convent. "What's the favor?"

"I'm just going to ask you to remember what's important."

Dad turns around and goes into the house. I suppose I'll have to work out the details with Mom. "Does this mean I can still see Patrick?"

"Of course."

I summon up my nerve and say, "Can I still kiss him?"

She nods and touches my hair the way she used to when I was small. "You're doing everything right, C.C. Believe it or not."

Mom gives me a kiss on the cheek and goes inside. I'm trying to imagine her relationship with her father when she was turning fifteen. She's been through this, I tell myself. And a bunch of other things I haven't been through yet. I smile at this weird but powerful image: Mother as Vanguard.

I go directly to my room where I pick up the phone and call Patrick.

"I'm not grounded," I tell him.

He's very relieved to hear this. Nevertheless, we decide to get together at his house tonight. All things considered, it's not a bad idea.

Outside, the leaves of my willow are whispering to me in the slowly softening light of what you'll have to agree has been a very strange day.

I just wish I knew what they were trying to say.

*   *   *

After dinner, Mr. O'Connell drives Pat over to pick me up. My dad doesn't tell me to take a coat, although I'm not sure if this can be thought of as progress. I grab the jean jacket anyway, because I know from experience that the O'Connells like to run their air conditioners at full throttle.

When we get to Pat's house, everyone is home. Danny and Ryan are playing Wiffle ball in the front yard. Mrs. O'Connell is inside with Mikey, who is already in his pajamas.

She offers me lemonade and asks my opinion of

a hairstyle she found in a magazine. Then she moves on to fabric swatches for the new living room curtains. She seems almost as thrilled as Patrick is to have me around, and I don't exactly blame her. The testosterone level in this household is lethal.

Ryan comes in groaning, with a scrape on his cheek the size of Wyoming. With four boys, Mrs. O'Connell is practically a paramedic. She disappears and returns with gauze pads and hydrogen peroxide to wash out Ryan's wound. The kid winces, but Mrs. O'Connell is made of steel. After the sterilization and bandaging process is complete, she rumples Ryan's hair and tells him to "Walk it off, kiddo." This does not reflect a lack of compassion. This is a mother comforting a son. My mother has never told me to walk off an injury.

I feel sort of sorry for Mrs. O'Connell, if you want to know the truth, and it's not just the toilet seat conspiracy, either. There was something about the way my mother touched my hair this afternoon that made me think she'd been waiting a long time to do it. Even though the circumstances were cruddy, I got the feeling we were making some very important connection. Sister Jude would have called it a rite of passage. The mom making sense of stuff for her teenage daughter; the daughter, at last, *needing* to have stuff make sense.

I remember a moment Mom and I had when I was seven, and I realize now that it was practice for the one we had today in the yard. We were in the attic, getting out Christmas decorations, and she came across a box of books from when she was a kid. I remember she got this weird, teary smile on her face, just before she handed me a worn copy of *Little Women*.

Watching Mrs. O'Connell as she's throwing away bloody gauze pads, I know that there's no one in this house who'd ever want her copy of *Little Women*—if she has one, which, I'd bet a million bucks, she does.

Pat is giving his mother a look indicating that we would like a little privacy. Mrs. O'Connell doesn't mind in the least. Emotionally speaking, I think mothers of sons have it easier than fathers of daughters.

We go into the family room. When we're alone in front of the TV, Pat takes my hand. "Happy anniversary," he says sweetly.

I give him a blank look, which I immediately regret because he looks crestfallen.

"Two months and three weeks today," he tells me.

"Oh. Right." My aunt and uncle celebrated their twenty-fifth anniversary last November; it was Silver. So two months and three weeks would be what? String?

He looks utterly serious, though, so I decide to dive for his lips. I'm about to, when we hear Danny cracking up from under the dining-room table.

"Get lost," Pat orders.

Danny disappears and I back off, too. A little brother watching from the dining room is the very definition of mood kill. Also, the AC is making my shoulders chilly, so I reach for Cluck's jean jacket and wrap it around my shoulders.

Pat gives the jacket a disapproving look. "Do you have to wear that all the time?"

"I don't wear it all the time," I answer. "I'm wearing it now because I'm cold."

"It's Cluck's."

"So?"

Pat gives a rough sigh. "I don't like you wearing something that he's worn."

I suppose I should find this adorable, but to tell you the truth, I'm amazed at how ridiculous it sounds.

"It's like he's here—between us," he adds, frowning.

I roll my eyes and assure him that it's not like that at all to me.

Patrick grumbles and picks up the remote control. He flips through the TV channels, and we end up watching some old movie in which the girl, deep down, wants to be a cheerleader.

This bores me nearly to tears and I decide to give making out another shot. Pat's willing. (Big surprise). After a while, I become aware of his hand, moving on its stealth mission toward my chest. The jean jacket acts as a shield, but Pat is undaunted. His hand moves to the upper pocket— and there's the sudden sound of paper crinkling inside. I have to laugh; it's as if the paper is some kind of alarm. I stop fast, though, because it is clear that Pat finds the laughter annoying.

I suppose he figures he has to disengage the security system in order to continue his mission, because the next thing he does is remove the piece of paper. And read it!

Mother of God, as Natalie would say.

Pat looks up from Tim Sinclair's European address and into my eyes. I'm wondering how we moved from second base to search and seizure—

he didn't even have probable cause, let alone a warrant.

"Why do you have Tim Sinclair's address in your pocket?" Patrick demands. He leans away from me, his eyes wild.

I can't tell if he's mad or hurt or what. So I give him a line that could have come right out of the dumb movie. "It isn't what you think."

"What is it then? And when did he give this to you?" Pat waves the paper in my face. "Was it last night at the Sinclairs' house, when you disappeared upstairs for so long?"

"Actually, it was this morning."

He's on his feet. "When, this morning?"

"Eight A.M., give or take," I say. "I needed a ride." I realize I'm cowering and decide that this is not the proper body language for the situation. I sit up straighter and life my chin. After all, I'm completely innocent—except maybe for the hug, and, as I said, it was not romantic in the least.

Pat's fuming now. "You needed a *ride* at eight in the morning? Where to?"

"It wasn't so much *to* as *from* . . ."

"From. . . ?"

"Football camp. It was an emergency."

Now Patrick is pacing, and, let me tell you,

jealousy-induced pacing is a rough activity. He shoves a rocking chair out of his path and kicks a pile of Mikey's stuffed animals. "You had a football camp emergency at eight o'clock in the morning? And what the heck does that have to do with you sneaking around with Tim's address?"

I feel my spine stiffen. "Sneaking around?" He's the one reaching into people's pockets! I'm about to mention that, but he goes on.

"Tim doesn't even go to football camp, C.C." He gives me a wicked look. "Maybe you should try a little harder to keep your *lies* straight."

I could save myself here and tell him about Grace spending the night with Billy Dennon, and her mom's brakes, and everything else. But I don't want to be the one to trash Grace's reputation, and, I don't appreciate Patrick giving me the third degree. More important, I don't like being called a liar.

"Why were you at football camp?" he demands.

"I had a good reason," I say firmly.

"This good reason," Pat snarls. "What's his name? Does *he* mind that you're messing around with Tim Sinclair?"

My eyes go wide with shock. "If that's what you really think, then we have nothing more to talk about," I tell him.

Pat throws himself into a chair at the opposite side of the room, and we do not say one more word to each other. At 11:26, I hear my father's car in the driveway. I jump off the couch and run for the door.

Pat stops me with a "Hey . . ."

"What?" I'm fully expecting him to throw his arms around me and apologize for not trusting me. Which is why I'm so surprised when he says, "I don't think this is working anymore."

Loosely translated, "this isn't working" means that Patrick O'Connell is breaking up with me. My stomach feels as if it's been stabbed by an ice pick. My eyes are stinging and I can barely make my mouth work enough to say, "Fine." I step out onto the front porch and Pat slams the door behind me.

I manage to say hello to my father when I get into the car, then I sort of crunch myself up against the door.

"What's wrong?"

"Pat and I broke up," I answer.

Then the tears start. I put my face against the window and cry all the way home. When we pull into the driveway, though, neither of us moves. I get the distinct impression that my father has something to say—or wishes he did. I glance at him, but he's staring at the steering wheel, and he looks completely and utterly overwhelmed. I'm not sure if it's because he doesn't know what to do, or if it's because he *does* know what to do, but is just afraid to do it.

I find myself wanting to hug him and tell him every word, but, of course, I'm just as scared as he is. And then I understand. Right here, right now, my dad and I are experiencing different parts of the same incredible helplessness. And although it is helplessness, we share it—so there is some comfort in that. I know that although we've never been farther apart, we've never been closer either. The confusion, the disagreements, fade like the end of a season, and we meet, just in time to leave each other.

We still don't move. I have this strange feeling that my father is holding me, but at the same time he's—what? Nudging me? Urging me on? *Loving* me away because it's time. Not according to some made-up schedule, like Pat's, but because this is natural, instinctive, and that makes it even harder. It's not a choice. It's just time.

My father is silent, holding me and urging me on with his heart. And that's when I notice. Dad is crying, too.

In my mind, at this moment, I finish his poem—

the one I started a lifetime ago at Sal Malanconico's pool party. When we finally go inside, I head straight for my room and write it down in my journal.

LEAVING MY FATHER
Summer has blasted the young daylight
to burning dusk.
Serpent air slithers, white-blue, wet-hot.
But the willow remembers
ice-drunkenness, a silver-plate frost,
dry cold swollen in its twig-yellow tents.

You have been winter
at my side, frozen against me,
storming snowy revelations, like January's wrath.

While I crouch,
a bulb of warmth,
ripening in hardened soil.

We are not one season,
and you, a sudden chill in the heat of this equinox,
love your child away.

Chapter 11————

At twelve-fifteen, I hear something I haven't heard in a long time: Cluck knocking on my window. I'm wide awake (who could sleep?). When I see Cluck, I feel instantly thankful, like somebody who's drowning and has just had a life preserver thrown to her.

I let him in and the first thing he says is, "You were crying."

"Patrick broke up with me."

"Patrick broke up with you?"

"Patrick broke up with me."

"When?"

"Just before. At his house."

"Why?"

I sit down on my bed. "Because Tim Sinclair gave me his address in Europe."

Cluck considers this. "Before or after he drove you home from football camp?"

I narrow my eyes at him. "I didn't tell you he gave me a ride."

Cluck smiles.

"How did you know?"

He leans against my dresser and picks up a little teddy bear he gave me in fourth grade. "I was there."

"Excuse me," I say, folding my arms across my chest, "but you most certainly were *not* there."

"Yes I was."

"You *deserted* us!" I suddenly remember that I'm angry with him. "You left us alone. With four trillion jocks. Do you know what could have happened?"

Cluck shrugs, studying the bear. "I dunno . . . you could've gotten whistled at, maybe? Or maybe Nat could've wrangled herself another T-shirt."

I blink.

"I was there, C.C."

"But I saw you leave."

"I wouldn't leave you, C.C.," he says, and his face is serious. "I wouldn't know how. When you were ten steps down the driveway, I hid in the bushes and kept an eye on you till you found Tim. I just didn't feel like dealing with Grace."

"But you did feel like letting Nat and me *think* you left us alone."

"That was low," Cluck admits, and a tiny smile crosses his face. "I guess I just wanted you to know how it feels."

"When are *you* ever alone?" I ask. "You're *never* alone."

He puts the bear back on the dresser and sits beside me. "Whenever I'm not with you, C.C., I'm alone."

These words send an electrical charge through me—twice the voltage of Pat's "I love you." I have to pause and take a breath.

"Why didn't you tell us at Sal's what happened with Grace and Billy?" I ask. "Everyone thought you were a jerk."

"I only cared what *you* thought," he tells me. "And why put Grace through that? Everybody knows how Billy is." (How Billy Is, I imagine, is the complete opposite of How I Am.) Cluck looks a little sad, I guess for Grace.

"So you were just protecting her reputation?" Admirable.

"Yeah." Cluck closes his eyes. "And mine. I'd already been thrown over by you for Pat . . ."

"I never threw you over."

He gives me this let's-not-get-into-it look and

sighs. "Anyway, you were worth it. Grace wasn't."

"Weren't you in love with her?" I ask.

"I liked her," he answers. "I liked her enough to kiss her—"

"A lot," I remind him. "You kissed her a lot."

"It's a guy thing."

"Of course."

"But I didn't love her. That's why we never . . . I mean, she wanted to . . . at least, she said she wanted to, but . . ."

"Is that why she chased down Billy?" This shocks me. "To. . . ?"

"That's my best guess." Cluck is genuinely unruffled.

I don't mind saying that I'm totally confused. Hadn't Grace led Nat and me to believe that she had used up most of her virginity with *Cluck?* Billy Dennon's name certainly never came up!

I bounce this off Cluck, who shakes his head.

"There's no such thing as mostly, C.C."

"So she just made it up?"

Cluck shrugs. "Who cares?"

Suddenly I'm very tired, so I put my head on Cluck's shoulder, and what's surprising is that neither of us finds it surprising at all. It's instinctive.

Cluck strokes my hair. There's something about having his arms around me that falls somewhere between new and familiar. (It's nothing like the brotherly hug I got from Tim; this hug's got juice.) Cluck kisses the top of my head, and I feel very safe, drifting toward a dream. *I am walking down the block, just about to turn the corner, and I can hear the scrape of the sidewalk beneath my sandals; it's a perfect, summery, blue-lit day . . .*

I'm not sure how long I've been sleeping, but when I wake up, Cluck is still here, stroking my hair.

"Cluck?"

"Yow?"

"What about Kelly?"

"She's Kelly."

"Right." I give him a sleepy smile. "It's a guy thing."

Cluck laughs. It's a new laugh for Cluck—sexy as ever, but gentle. Soft.

"How long was I sleeping?"

He shrugs and checks my clock. "An hour."

"An *hour?*"

He nods.

"What have you been doing?"

"Watching you."

"Watching me? For a whole *hour?*"

"I'm good at it, C.C. I've been watching you forever."

And all of a sudden, I remember. I remember so completely that I can't even believe I forgot. The day I walked to Natalie's house in my sandals, Cluck was sitting on his front porch. The hazy part of my memory . . . it was *Cluck.* He was watching me; Cluck is what made the terror go away.

I smile, and he wants to know why.

"I was just remembering these sandals I had when I was six. You probably wouldn't remember . . ."

"White sandals. Green daisies. Three straps."

And it's at this moment that I understand, beyond all doubt, that no one will ever be in love with me the way Gilbert McNally is in love with me. So I kiss him.

And he kisses me. It's soft and slow and electric and shimmery, and it feels like a kiss he's been waiting for all his life. What I discover now is that I've been waiting for this kiss, too.

He pauses long enough to whisper a very small "Yow," then he kisses me again. I've never been so scared and so *not* scared in my whole, entire life. And I realize that I'm about to turn another corner, a different kind of corner.

But Cluck's here. So I know it's all right.

I tell Nat because I have to. She's my best friend.
It's in our contract.

"You're kidding!"

But I'm not, of course. It's late Wednesday afternoon. We are on lawn chairs in my back yard,
checking out Nat's latest haul of catalogues and
magazines.

"What about Grace?"

"He never loved her."

Nat gives me a funny look. "You thought he
loved her?"

"Didn't you?"

"C.C.," she says, flipping a page in her magazine, "you are far too sophisticated and much too
good-looking to be so naive."

I decide not to quibble over the fact that you
can't grammatically justify calling someone
sophisticated and naive in the same sentence,
except maybe in a poem. "What does that mean?"

"Come on."

"Come on what?"

"C.C. It's *Cluck*."

"Yes," I remind her, "we've met."

"Cluck loves only you. Always has, always will."
She cracks this small smile to let me know she's

144

teasing when she adds, "How greedy can you get?"

Greedy? What does she mean, greedy? I ask, "What do you mean, greedy?"

"I mean, Cluck, Patrick, Tim, Sal Malanconico."

"I never kissed Sal Malanconico. And I never kissed Tim."

"But you could have."

"What's your point? Aren't *you* the one harboring an entire athletic department's-worth of jerseys and T-shirts in your closet?" This, by the way, is not a fight. This is Nat and me expressing ourselves freely and openly, confident in the knowledge that we're best friends. "Aren't *you* the one who won't give poor Frankie Bruno a straight answer?"

Oops—think I hit a nerve. The look on her face is a combination of shame and grief.

"What?" I say quickly. "I was only kidding."

"I know. But it's true." She folds down the corner of a page featuring step-by-step instructions for tweezing flawless brows. "I *want* to tell Frankie I like him."

"So . . ." Seems like a no-brainer to me. "Tell him."

Nat gives me a smile, then an eye roll. "I'm not you, C.C. I'm different from you."

"You've got more belts," I concede. "But—"

"I'm different from you because you're different from everyone. You've got this power to keep boys interested."

She's probably referring to Cluck's eleven-year crush. "You're exaggerating," I tell her. "I'm not powerful, I'm lucky."

Nat is shaking her head. "It's not luck. It's something else. If Frankie knew I really liked him, he'd get bored. Wish fulfillment, and all that. You know."

I don't, actually. Nat's the mind reader in this relationship; I usually need clarification.

"If Frankie *thinks* he's got to wait for me, he will," she says, patiently. "The T-shirts are just a visual aid."

I turn the concept over in my mind, and it occurs to me that maybe Nat doesn't realize how terrific she is. "Trust Frankie," I tell her. "Sometimes that works."

We read in silence for a while. Then Nat says she's got to go home. She doesn't say why, but I know she wants to be there in case Frankie calls—so maybe my mind-reading capabilities are finally kicking in. I also know that Frankie *will* call, but this is not based on ESP; this is based on a working knowledge of teenage boys, Frankie Bruno in particular.

When Nat's gone, I open my journal to the poem that I began at Sal's house, the poem for my father. I copy it onto a separate piece of paper; then, at the top of the page, beneath the title, I write *For Charles Carruthers.*

When I look up, my dad is coming into the back yard, holding an express-delivery package. Actually, in one hand he's holding an express-delivery package—an *opened* express-delivery package.

In the other, he's holding the date bra.

Chapter 12 ─────

"You opened it?"

"I . . ."

"You opened *my mail!*" I will not deny that I'm hysterical. But my father is standing there, less than twenty feet away, and he's holding a sheer black bra with lace accents, which happens to belong to me. I'm entitled to be hysterical, wouldn't you say?

"I opened it because it was addressed to C. Carruthers." Dad shakes the bra at me, then looks as if he wishes he hadn't. "*I* happen to be C. Carruthers, too."

"Didn't you check the return address?" I jump up from the lawn chair. "Since when do you get lingerie in the mail?"

"Since when do you?" Good one.

I pick up my journal and prepare to storm past

my father and into the house. As luck would have it, however, Gilbert "Cluck" McNally picks this extremely unfortunate moment to appear around the side of the house.

"Yow."

My dad tries to stuff the bra back into the cardboard delivery envelope, but it won't go. He's stuck with it.

Cluck looks at me and I look at him; then he looks at my father, who is looking at me *and* holding a sheer black bra with lace accents, which may very well be the absolute sexiest bra in the history of underwear. Cluck takes a good look at that bra. I can only imagine what he's thinking: *C.C. ordered sexy lingerie and got caught.* Or, *Mr. Carruthers is a cross-dresser.* Or, *Hey, Kelly has that exact same bra.*

My father's face is purple, but I can't tell if this is from fury or embarrassment. As for me, I can't even begin to explain what it feels like to have both your father *and* the boy who was once your best friend but is now your potential official boyfriend viewing your date bra for the first time. Viewing your date bra for the first time *simultaneously.*

It's a nightmare. *A nightmare.*

But Dad has finally managed to get the bra

tucked back into the envelope. He looks far less ridiculous now.

Cluck says, "Yow, Mr. Carruthers."

"Yow, Cluck."

"Yow, C.C."

I say, "Hi."

"Wanna go for sodas?" That's Cluck—grace under pressure; never let 'em see you sweat.

At this point, my father decides to take the envelope and its contents into the house, probably to set them on fire. All things considered, ask me if I care.

Cluck and I start walking. "Nice bra," he says.

"Shut up."

These are the last words we speak till we get to the burger place. I'm happy to see that it's not especially crowded. Cluck orders two Cokes. Then he looks at me very calmly and says, "Now what?"

"Now what?"

He nods. (Cluck has eaten dinner at my house with my parents five zillion times, and this is the first time Now What has ever come up.)

I say, "Now what, what?"

"I'm kind of scared."

"You're not scared of anything," I tell him, and I know this for a fact.

"I was scared to kiss you behind the baptismal font in second grade," he reminds me.

The other boys in our communion class had dared him to try that little bit of sacrilege; when he hadn't, they'd made chicken noises at him, and that's how he got his nickname. I didn't know that until recently, though. Only Gilbert McNally could turn an insult into one of the coolest nicknames in town.

"And," he says, "I was scared at Sal Malanconico's when Pat said he loved you."

"Yeah, well . . . he doesn't love me anymore."

"I loved you first," says Cluck.

I sip my Coke. "Do you love me last?" (This, of course, is the real question.)

He smiles. It's better than any smile anyone has ever gotten from any boy ever. "I'm gonna marry you, C.C."

"So you've said." (Seventy-eight billion times since kindergarten.) I give him a smile that I hope is the girl version of his.

"But . . ."

"*But. . . ?*"

Cluck shrugs. "I need time."

"Time?" It's not as if I expect him to marry me *now,* right after we finish our Cokes. What does he mean, time?

Cluck drags his hands through his hair. "I told you, I'm scared. Getting what you want is damn scary, C.C."

If he's talking about sexy lingerie from a mail-order catalogue, I'm inclined to agree. But he's not; he's talking about me. I'm so floored that I don't even have a "don't cuss" in me. "It's not as if you haven't had eleven years to prepare for it."

Cluck shrugs. "That's sort of the point."

Now my heart is pounding; there is a boulder in my throat. There's a word Sister Jude taught us in freshman English. *Denouement.* It's the literary term for events that come after the climax of a story, in which the resolution takes place. In case you're not following me, Cluck and me kissing last night was the climactic point in our relationship. Now we're rolling toward resolution. But I have this horrible feeling that it's not going to be the resolution I was expecting.

"So you're saying you don't want to—"

Cluck stops me by shaking his head. "I'm just saying that, right this second, I'm scared."

"When will you not be scared?" I ask him.

He answers with another shrug.

Is this out of the blue, or what? Not to mention completely unfair and a little insane. I have this stupid idea that if I remind him about the black bra with the lace accents, I might be able to change his mind. But every one of Nat's magazines advises women not to use sex as a weapon. I never really understood that before, but I'm beginning to see how the opportunity could present itself.

Then Cluck leans across the booth and kisses me full on the lips. This is not a guy thing. This is not even a Catholic thing. This is a *Cluck* thing.

He gets up from the table. "Bye, babe."

And this is when I remember the derivation of the word *denouement:* from the Old French *desnouement,* an untying; *desnour,* to undo.

Don't ever let anyone tell you that you won't use freshman English in real life. Because, believe me, you will.

* * *

I spend Wednesday night reading my journal. I go all the way back to the beginning; sixth grade, when it used to be my Curtis Journal and I was his biggest fan. Somewhere around the middle is that French kiss, which pretty much started it all.

At the time, it seemed unforgettable. At the moment, I can barely remember it. Four lips, two tongues, a lot of saliva—the usual. Unlike the kiss

Cluck gave me last night, which I can actually still feel on my lips. Don't believe me, I don't care; but that is the God's honest truth: I can feel it. There's this echo, this ghost of a kiss, and it's not just on my lips. It's in my heart.

As far as I can tell, I am in love with Gilbert McNally. That's the only explanation.

* * *

On Thursday morning, I decide I can no longer stand withholding poetry from Sister Jude. It's making me too lonely. So I grab my journal and start walking. But the closer I get to school, the more nervous I feel. This is because I cannot, in good conscience, share my new poems with Sister until I find out why she has defected to the cheerleaders.

There's got to be a reason. Maybe she's shooting for martyrdom. Or perhaps she's determined to adjust the rhyme schemes of some of their cheers. Or maybe, deep down, Sister Jude—like Grace Boccaluzzo—wants to be part of the giggling elite.

I find Sister on the side lawn.

"Hello, C.C.!"

I smile but can't manage a "hi," and this is because I'm choked up. I am choked up over the fact that Sister Jude is sincerely happy to see me.

I was afraid the cheerleaders might have poisoned her against me.

She looks at the journal. "Poetry?"

I nod, but don't give it to her.

"You okay?" she asks.

"I'm just turning a corner," I tell her.

"Corners are tough." She sighs.

"Sister, may I ask you something?" I take a deep breath, bracing myself. "Why did you take over as pep squad advisor? Did you break one of your vows? Is this your punishment?"

At this, Sister Jude cracks up. I mean, really cracks up. Insanity is now on my list of possible reasons.

"C.C.," she says, getting hold of herself, "I took the position because they needed a coach. Sister Maureen is going off with the missionaries next term, and of all the faculty, I had the most free time in my schedule."

I blink. "So this isn't about penance, or atonement?"

"Actually, it's more about keeping my job."

They needed a coach. Period. I can't begin to describe my relief.

"Mind if *I* ask *you* a question?" says Sister.

"No. Go ahead."

"What do you think about cheerleaders?"

I smile in spite of myself. Less than a week ago, I was asking Patrick the same question. "I think I'm supposed to want to be one."

"But you don't."

I shake my head.

"C.C., it's easy to spot the cheerleaders."

"Yeah, well, the uniforms and all . . ."

She gives my journal a tap. "Go to a football game sometime, though, and see if you can spot the poets. Do you understand?"

I nod. I do. *Independence.*

Sister Jude smiles. There's a heavenly sort of kindness in it, no kidding.

"You wouldn't last five minutes in a cheerleading uniform, C.C.," she tells me. And I know she's right. Not only do I not want to be a cheerleader— I don't even want to *want* to be a cheerleader. That's what was bothering me before, of course. I wanted to want to be a cheerleader, but I just couldn't dredge up the enthusiasm.

But now . . . well, in plain English, the hell with it!

Suddenly, I don't even hate the cheerleaders anymore. Not in any general sense, that is. Kelly will always work my nerves, but now I understand that it's not because she can punch up a mean handspring. It's really just because she's Kelly.

A pleasant stillness passes between Sister and me. I've never felt so utterly relieved in my life— so free. I give Sister the journal, and she flips to the pages where the new poems start. The sun is warm across my shoulders, and I drift away to a dazy, non-cheerleadery place, which is why, when Sister Jude reads the words, ". . . to commit what will remain there in the heat," I blurt out, "It sounded better than 'second base.'"

My hand flies to my mouth. I just said "second base" to a nun. Am I looking to get myself excommunicated, or what?

But Sister is laughing. "Anything sounds better than 'second base.'"

"You know what that means?" This is unbelievable. Talking to a nun about getting felt up is right up there with having your father find your date bra.

She nods. "I've always thought that the baseball metaphor is just plain dumb."

"Me, too."

I look beyond Sister, across the side lawn. Ironically, I have a very clear view of the softball field, and suddenly, I imagine myself there, running toward first base—running fast because I really want to get there. I stop on the bag, and I'm satisfied. But the invisible crowd is cheering me on, screaming for me to keep going.

"I think I know what's wrong with it."

"Tell me," says Sister.

"In baseball, you don't get any points for getting to first. You aren't allowed to enjoy it! You're supposed to round first and keep sprinting for second, then third. If you don't, you lose the game. But sex isn't a game. There isn't a scorekeeper somewhere who's going to pencil in an error if I decide to stop at kissing, is there?"

"Not that I know of," Sister Jude says, grinning. "I think that's part of why you find the baseball terms offensive—because in your heart, C.C., you know it's not a game."

"I think people think it is."

She laughs. It's a sad kind of laugh, very poetic. "They do. And they shouldn't."

Something dawns on me now. "Maybe people think that if they talk about it like it's a game, it'll feel like a game. Maybe calling it what it is, is just too scary."

"You're probably correct, C.C. But I suspect when it's right, it gets a lot less scary."

"When is it right?" I ask quickly and a bit desperately. "It's hard to wait. It's hard not to wait. So when is it right?"

"Oh," Sister says, with an easy shrug, "I suppose it's different for everyone."

See, now; I always thought the Church had a very clear position on this.

Sister Jude hands me back my journal. Then I thank her for her advice, and she tells me to stop by when I've got more poems.

"God bless you, C.C.," she calls after me.

We start off in opposite directions, and I can't help remembering those catalogues she was carrying on the last day of school. I figure the new cheerleading sweaters will be arriving at St. Bernie's any day now. They're probably costing the athletic department a small fortune. For all I know, they're being shipped via the same carrier that delivered my date bra. I wonder vaguely if Sister will think of me when she opens the box.

Of course, she and I both know that even if every one of those sweaters were exactly my size, there wouldn't be one in the box that would ever fit me.

And you know what? I wouldn't have it any other way.

Chapter 13————————

I'm ready for Lisa Bruno's party. I'm not wearing the date bra. What would be the point? My father drives me to Lisa's and pulls up to the curb. I hope he isn't planning to ask me if Mr. and Mrs. Bruno are home. No one is making out on the front lawn, which works in my favor.

"Thanks for the ride."

"You're welcome."

These, I should mention, are practically the first words we've spoken since the bra incident. I take a folded piece of paper out of my pocket and hand it to him.

"What's this?"

"A poem. For you. I wrote it."

He looks surprised. Then sad. Then scared. Then curious. I must look all those things, too. He unfolds it with the same care Sister Jude generally takes when accepting a poem.

Dad's voice is a little thin. "Should I read it?"

I shrug, then nod. "Yeah," I tell him. "You should read it."

He takes a deep breath, and I can't blame him. Reading a poem written for you by your teenage daughter is attempting a triple reverse gainer off the emotional high dive. I follow his eyes, remembering the way he would study the finger painting masterpieces I used to bring home from kindergarten. Suddenly, in spite of the fact that he's sitting two feet away in the driver's seat, I miss him.

After a minute or two I ask, "Do you understand it?"

"I think so." He quotes me: "We are not one season."

"Right." I'm quick to clarify. "But that's not intended as an insult."

"I know." Dad reaches over and touches my hair; it's different from the way Mom did. Not better or worse, just different. It's part apology, part promise.

I get out of the car and Dad says, "C.C. . . ."

"Yes?"

"It all works out," he tells me. "Sooner or later, it all works out."

I'm not sure what he means, exactly. Me and him? Me and Cluck? Both, maybe. That would be nice. Dad smiles, and I guess he's not exactly sure either. But he wants things to work out, and I suppose that's half the battle. Suddenly, I wish I could apologize—not for the last couple of days, but for the next couple. And for the days after that, too, because I know there are going to be more tough moments between us. They won't be my fault, and they won't be his. They'll just be. It's normal. Painful, but normal.

So I don't apologize. I just wave. Dad waves, too, then drives away. It feels a little like the day I walked to Nat's in my sandals.

I run into Curtis and Bridget first, because they're arguing (what else is new?) on the Brunos' front porch. I go inside. Sal Malanconico gives me this huge hug. This is my first indication that The News Is Out. I'm no longer Patrick O'Connell's girl-friend, and that makes it open season on hugging.

I say, "Hi, Sal," and go directly to Patrick, who's sitting in the kitchen looking very tortured. It's a good look for Patrick; my guess is, he's already been hugged by every female in the room.

"Still mad?" I ask.

He shakes his head. "Cluck explained about

Grace and Billy and the whole football camp thing." I know he wants to get back together, because he gives me one of our inside-joke looks. Guess what? It does nothing for me.

Pat says, "We need to talk. In private."

What he actually means is, let's go somewhere where we can start talking and end up kissing. It's the part of Pat's agenda that falls under the heading of reconciliation: a heart-to-heart conversation followed by major making out.

I shake my head.

He pulls out the big guns and gives me that almost-smile that used to work. "Are you sure?"

"I'm sure." I'm not playing hard to get, either. Tonight, *I* have an agenda. "You broke up with me," I remind him and add this little huff I learned from Nat. (It's a girl thing.)

"We can unbreak up."

"There's no such thing."

Pat gives me a very tortured sigh. "Is it Tim?"

"It never was. I told you that."

"Is it Cluck?" He looks me straight in the eye for this one. "Is it?"

"I think so." (I'm being as honest as I can.) "I think it will be."

"Was it always Cluck, C.C.?"

I'm thinking: *Definitely.* Of course, I've only recently realized this, and admitting it to Pat would be just plain cruel. Honesty is one thing. But there's no need to get nasty. So I say, "No. It was definitely you while it was you."

This soothes him somewhat. We're quiet for a moment.

Pat says, "I'll always love you, C.C."

Maybe it's the truth. But then, maybe it's just what Pat thinks he's supposed to say. In either case, it's a great exit line. So I take off to find Natalie.

I spot her on a couch, making out with Frankie. "Hi, Nat."

She comes up for air and says, "Grace made cheerleading."

"Get out."

"It gets even better. Guess who's her new best friend." Natalie gives me the quintessential eye roll.

I laugh. Then I bend down and whisper very matter-of-factly in Frankie's ear, "She's crazy about you. The shirts are just shirts." Next, I lean across Frankie and whisper in Natalie's ear, "Trust him."

After that I leave so they can go back to making out.

I find Grace in the back yard, celebrating with Kelly and Lisa. (Best friends in less than a day—

think it'll last?) When Grace sees me, she whispers something to them, and they all start giggling like crazy.

This cinches it; the inside cover of my yearbook is obsolete. I guess once a girl like Grace gets her first pair of pompoms, nothing else matters. I'm not especially astounded, but I am hurt. She never even thanked me for risking my life (or, at the very least, my virtue) to get her out of football camp. She didn't take any of it seriously—not being in bed with Billy, not being rescued by her friends. But it was hugely serious to me. And here's where I realize that Grace has a very different definition of friendship than I do. My version, like Cluck's and Nat's, has to do with loyalty and respect. Hers has to do with uniforms, and living up to stupid expectations that make people blend into one another.

I look for Cluck for forty-three minutes before I conclude that he has not come to Lisa Bruno's party. This throws me. Cluck has been at every party I've ever been to in my life, with the exception of Kelly's eighth birthday, but he would have looked dumb in an upsweep.

I'm filled with an entirely new caliber of loneliness. It's not even nine o'clock, but suddenly, I have to go home. I interrupt Nat again to tell her I've got to leave immediately. I don't have to tell her why. She's my best friend; she just knows.

Curtis and Bridget are still on the front porch. Judging from the way she's plastered up against him and the way his hands are practically on her butt, I figure they've put aside their differences.

When I'm halfway down the Brunos' walk, I hear them behind me. They're strolling down the path, holding hands; they're not following me, we just happen to be going in the same direction.

Curtis says, "Going home, C.C.?"

I nod. They fall into step beside me, and Bridget, in an impressive show of maturity, doesn't look at all uncomfortable. I realize that I don't know much about her.

A brief discussion of the party follows.

"I liked the music," Curtis says.

"Too many cheerleaders," Bridget says, and I smile.

There's something about the way Curtis is looking at her. I know that look. I should—it's the way Cluck looked at me for eleven years (before he decided he needed time, that is). And this is when the analogy hits me: *Bridget is to Curtis as C.C. is to Cluck!* There are undeniable similarities when you think about it. By the end of this walk, I'm convinced that Curtis will love Bridget forever.

We part company on the sidewalk in front of Curtis's house, and when I say to Bridget, "See you at the burger place," it sounds a little like an invitation. You know something? After tonight, I think I could actually pull off having a soda with Bridget Glenn and not even choke. I might even enjoy it.

Crossing my lawn, I'm trying to remember if Patrick ever looked at me the way Cluck looked at me, or the way Curtis looked at Bridget. I conjure up a lot of scenes; the first time we kissed, and the first time he said "I love you," for example. In all of these scenes, Pat is looking at me with interest. But interest isn't what I'm talking about. I'm talking about something soft and nameless and instinctive. Something that would make it impossible for him to bounce from "I love you" to "This isn't working" with such reckless abandon.

It occurs to me that Patrick was merely proceeding according to his plan; it was *time* to be in love with me. This is perfectly in character, because basically, doing things utterly right is Pat's trademark. I don't mean that he was lying—I'm sure he felt something. He even may have been on the brink of loving me. And when I told him that I loved him at the burger place I wasn't exactly lying either. I cared for him—and I suppose I always will. (You can't kiss a guy that much without developing *some* lasting connection.) But I know now that I didn't love him. In all honesty, I was just trying to keep up.

I go in the house and straight to my room, where I find Cluck lying on my bed.

"Hi, babe."

First, I almost drop dead from shock. Then I say, "What the hell are you doing here?"

Cluck says, "Don't cuss." He's not about to make this easy.

"I looked for you at Frankie's," I tell him, sitting down on the bed. "Then I remembered. You Need Time." There are only six tons of sarcasm in that statement.

He sits up and touches my hair. "I hear Patrick wants to get back together with you."

"That's *his* problem."

"Is it?" Cluck uses his sexiest voice for this, and I don't mind saying it makes my heart quiver. I'm beginning to regret that I am not wearing the date bra. Cluck has already seen it, but I get the feeling it would have an entirely different effect under the present circumstances.

He takes my face in his hands. It's a sophisticated move. He kisses my cheek first, then goes

168

for my lips. It's a repeat of Tuesday night's kiss.

"Does this mean time's up?" I ask.

"We need to talk."

"Go ahead."

"I've waited eleven years for you to love me, C.C. And now you do."

"Isn't that what you wanted?"

Cluck nods. He holds up my journal, which clearly he has been reading. My first instinct is to pound him, but then I realize that Cluck already knows everything about me anyway. Plus, I happen to be in love with him.

"You and Curtis," he says. "You and Pat. You and Tim."

This is sounding familiar. "I never kissed Tim."

"That's not the point." Cluck shrugs. "Me and Kelly. Me and Grace. Me and Kelly."

Now I see what he's getting at. The statistics are kind of grim. I suppose his theory was, if we weren't together, we couldn't come apart.

He pulls me close and I feel him trembling. Cluck, in case you're wondering, is not ordinarily a trembler. I hold him. Everything rugged about him is suddenly fragile. "*That's* what scared me, C.C." He releases me to drag his hand through his hair. (Very Cluck.) Then he turns to a poem in the journal—

"Tonight in Captivity"—and in his smokiest voice, he quotes me.

"'It is a scene, not a moment. . . .'"

I don't know if you've ever been quoted by the boy you love, but, trust me, it's a very heady experience. I'm holding my breath, and my fingertips are practically itching to touch him, to trace his lips and feel for my words.

He says the last line softly: ". . . I've forgotten you already."

I remember what I was thinking when I wrote that, and I know that Cluck understands. A scene is acted; it's outward. A moment is felt; it's real. "Patrick was a scene. You want to be a moment," I tell him.

He nods. "A moment, a lifetime . . . I can't let you forget me."

I quote *him* now: "I wouldn't know how."

"I kissed you the other night," he whispers, as if he still can't believe it.

"I was there," I remind him, smiling. I'm not sure if he's still scared, so I ask, "Are you going to kiss me again?"

He assures me he will. I tell him I'd like it in writing. I hand him a pen and wait while he writes in the journal.

"So you do love me?"

"C.C., I couldn't not love you." (Finally, a double negative I can live with.)

He looks at me in that soft, nameless, instinctive way. "So we're together," he tells me.

We've been together, I am thinking, for eleven years. But I don't have to tell you that this is a new and improved together. This together is serious. And since it's Cluck and I can ask him anything, I do.

"Promise me we won't use the baseball thing."

"Deal."

"And promise we won't rush. We won't do anything until it's . . ."

". . . until it's right," he finishes. (I'm glad he said "right" and not "time." Those two things really have nothing to do with each other.)

Then Cluck says he'd better go, and when he climbs out the window I'm right behind him. We kiss in the moonlight for a long time. Then I walk him around to the front and stand at the end of the driveway while he heads home.

"Night, C.C.," he says.

And I whisper so only the stars can hear me. "Bye, babe."

I watch him go. I watch him all the way to the corner, and even after he turns it and disappears across his front lawn and into his house. I miss him instantly, and I suppose that's silly. I mean, I'm going to see him at the burger place tomorrow. It's just that I'm going to see him differently at the burger place tomorrow. And if you don't know what I'm talking about, then you've never been in love with someone like Cluck.

Or, then again, maybe you've been in love with someone like Cluck all your life, and you just didn't know it. Because that kind of thing can actually happen. Believe me.

It can happen.